Southern
Gothic

Southern Gothic

edited by
**Brian Centrone
& Jordan M. Scoggins**

Also by New Lit Salon Press

I Voted for Biddy Schumacher: Mismatched Tales from the Mind of Brian Centrone
Retrospective by Michael Tice
Erotica by Brian Centrone
Behind the Yellow Wallpaper: New Tales of Madness edited by Rose Yndigoyen
Salon Style edited by Brian Centrone

Forthcoming

Startling Sci-Fi: New Tales of the Beyond edited by Casey Ellis

Published by New Lit Salon Press, 2014

© 2014 New Lit Salon Press

Line Edited by Casey Ellis
Digital collage art by Nathan Mark Phillips
Art Direction and Design by luke kurtis

Southern Gothic: New Tales of the South was originally published as an eBook in
October 2013 by New Lit Salon Press. A limited print edition was also published in
collaboration with bd-studios.com at the same time.

"The Phrenologist" was previously published under the same title in *The Southwestern
Review* (University of Southwestern Louisiana, now the University of Louisiana at
Lafayette), Volume 11 (1987).

New Lit Salon Press
Carmel, NY

Print ISBN 978-0-9885512-7-5 (this edition)
Print ISBN 978-0-9890266-1-1 (limited edition published with bd-studios.com)
eBook ISBN 978-0-9885512-2-0

www.newlitsalonpress.com

Table of Contents

Them Riders **7**
by Eryk Pruitt

Long Gone Girls **16**
by Rose Yndigoyen

Visitin' Cormierville **27**
by Hardy Jones

Windblown **39**
by Kent Tankersley

The Confession **47**
by Miranda Stone

Canaan **52**
by Caitlin Cauley

Tuesday Night Chorus **60**
by Heather Bell Adams

Two Poems **68**
by Emily Ruth Isaacson

A New Bike for Little Mike **73**
by Hardy Jones

Instrument **83**
by Mark Pritchard

Her Prince Charming **93**
by Zachary Honey

Snout of the Alligator **98**
by Charles J. Beacham

Love Like Dysphoria **107**
by A.G. Carpenter

Long Finger from the Sky **112**
by Michael Russell

A Sleeping Place **118**
by A.A. Garrison

The Phrenologist **125**
by Shane K. Bernard

Them
Riders

Eryk Pruitt

Wilbur Turgow dropped the dew-soaked newspaper and stared hell-fire toward the neighbor's yard. Not a split second later he stomped across the rust-stained patch of lawn separating their houses. He hoped to high heaven they heard his footsteps shouting across the way long before he made the front door, but felt vindicated when he had to ring the bell anyway. And ring he did. Over and over and over until—

"Mister Turgow," said Rhonda. Turgow wished the man had answered, as he never liked delivering fire and brimstone to a woman. But this weren't no ordinary woman.

"I think I done asked you folks to mind them weeds, didn't I?" he growled. "I done said time and time again to your husband to look after your yard."

"I beg your pardon, Mister Turgow," she began, but there never was any reaching him when he took this way.

"I done told you," he stammered. "See how them weeds grow up over my property, shitting seed and pollen all over my grass? I pay good money to take care of my side, I'll have you know."

"I reckon you do," she said, lowering her eyes.

Still, he would have none of it. "I don't reckon that neighborhood you moved from nobody gave nary a lick about the condition of their yard. Not the ilk running about those neighborhoods, do they? Well I tell you around here it's a different world. A much different world, I'll have you know."

She didn't bother asking him to explain. There was no mystery. To a man like Turgow, she and her husband could have been aliens, for all he cared. She fancied any black family would have the same issue in this corner of the world.

"You can get uppity all you want," he said. He thought to say more, but something far away caught his attention, if only for a moment. He listened, head cocked to the side like a mongrel dog catching a faint whiff of feline or something lame. He slowly turned his head to her and smiled, smiled as if suddenly blessed. She thought she'd sick up her lunch.

"Mister Turgow?" she asked.

"They'll come," he whispered. "They always do."

"I beg your—" She clutched her apron and wished Wendell would come walking up the way. "Who'll come, Mister Turgow?"

He flung brown juice from his lips, specked the edge of her front step. He didn't bother to stamp it with his foot.

"They like things a certain way in this town, you hear?" Behind him, bronzed beech leaves rattled like bones. He leaned closer. "They never did. They run out them big tobacco companies once. They run out the priest feller took to boys. And they going to run you folks out, plain and simple. They watch this town and they make sure don't nothing improper set foot in here. And if it do, they weed it out."

Her face caught fire and she cursed her eyes for burning, for betraying her in front of this man. She wished she could be strong and put the fear of something into him, wished to heaven Wendell would never find out. Wished she could take care of it. It'd been her who pushed Wendell to move here, her who insisted they leave that trash-strewn lot across town. They'd moved. They'd settled. And then Wilbur Turgow.

"Mister Turgow," she said evenly, "I'm going to ask you to step off my property. Do you hear me?"

He smiled that sick smile and again her stomach lurched. "I hear you good and proper," he said. He took a step back, then another. "You tell your husband what I said about them weeds. And you think about what I said about them riders. Because folks know when this town gets threatened, they come. You hear?"

He left and Rhonda let go of her apron for the first time in who knew how long.

Rhonda went down to the Minyard's for some milk and things; not the old one out on six-oh-one, but the newer one just put in by the hardware shop and the five-and-ten. She tramped up and down the aisles with a list of things in her head, but picked up nary an item because she was lost in the words of Wilbur Turgow. She'd run over in her head a few dozen times the deal about the riders before she heard Suzanne Warren crowing away in her ear.

"You deaf or something?" Suzanne went on and on. "I asked if you was okay?"

Rhonda nodded. "I'm so sorry," she said. "I must've been off in my own world. What was you saying?"

"I was saying that the way you carried on in the aisle here, you must be from another planet." Suzanne tinkered with her child in the front of her shopping cart, set the kid to, kept him from fidgeting through the basket of soup cans and toilet paper and boxes of ready-meals. "Heck, I bet you and me could have been talking an hour and you'd have never heard a word I said."

Rhonda's lips tightened at the edges and she waved her hand. *From another planet...* She hugged her groceries. Across the aisle, Bob Parson's wife looked through the cereal.

"I have had a horrible day," Rhonda said.

"Oh dear," said Suzanne. "Wendell's all right, ain't he?"

"Yes," said Rhonda. "Wendell's fine. Neighbor trouble. Wilbur Turgow."

"Ahh." Suzanne closed her eyes and nodded. She looked down the aisle. Bob Parson's wife moved along. "Never you mind him. He comes from another time. A time when folks like you and folks like me weren't supposed to shop in the same groceries. He's harmless. He can get agitated, sure, but he's harmless."

"Agitated is one thing," said Rhonda, "but Turgow is a mess. He said there was riders out there would tell me and Wendell what for."

Suzanne wiped the corners of her mouth with her thumb and forefinger. Her eyes darted to and fro. She opened her mouth to speak, but thought better of it. Bob Parson's wife made her way back onto the aisle, still eyeballing cereal boxes, or pretending to. Suzanne made a smile or what Rhonda hoped was a smile and touched her shoulder lightly. "Neighborhoods are like an Almond Joy, sweetheart: there's a nut in every cluster." She squeezed Rhonda's bicep tight and pushed the cart along, young one and all. Rhonda thought a moment before drawing her next breath.

Tears stinging her eyes, she paid for her groceries and shoved her own cart out the electric doors. This was not why she moved here. Kelman's had shops up and down the coast and she could have taken her pick, but she'd jumped at the chance to work at one so close to her mother, one smack dab in the middle of the new shopping center in town. Any town with a Kelman's was a town on the rise. Or so she told herself.

She stopped shy of lifting the trunk lid, let her head rest at her wrist a moment. She took it all in. Across the road were jackhammers, but on this side were robins, wrens, and the sound of children. Kids asking for candy or begging Mom to ride in the front seat or even kids on the mechanical horse out front that only cost a quarter. She thought about Wendell and what they could or couldn't do and where they may or may not be allowed to do it.

She thought about Kelman's and where the other shops were, and Suzanne came up from behind and put a hand on her elbow.

"Them riders ain't nothing but ghost stories," she whispered.

"I beg pardon."

"Ain't nothing but boogeyman talk they tell to keep folks in line," she said. She looked around the lot, made sure to keep the cart holding her boy at a straight-arm's length. She kept her voice low. "Sure, once a few men ran about making sure tobacco buyers was kept in line. Maybe later they chased out a few Germans or some Japs. I've heard stories about...I've heard stories. But that's what they are: stories."

"Wilbur Turgow ain't no story," said Rhonda and she meant it. "I've dealt with Wilbur Turgows my entire life."

"We all have," said Suzanne. "They come with the territory."

Rhonda wanted to tell her then *pity the territory*, but instead opened the trunk of her car and began stacking groceries. Suzanne pushed her own shopping cart back a step and leaned into Rhonda.

"Don't say no more about them riders," she whispered.

"What's that?"

"Them riders," hissed Suzanne. "You don't need to say no more about them. It won't do you no good."

Rhonda lowered her head. What more did anyone need to say? Suzanne squeezed her forearm as if to say all was okay, then went back to her child and her shopping cart full of wherewithals and wheeled off to her parking spot. Rhonda, when finished packing, slammed the trunk shut and got in the car.

"Ain't no use," she grumbled before turning the key in the ignition. Across the street, jackhammers chattered. "Not around here and not around nowhere. Ain't no use whatsoever."

She said nothing to Wendell that night. They went to bed after dinner none the wiser and she'd let herself forget, but came around sudden well past midnight when the sound of hoofbeats and hellfire brought her to.

"What's that?" screamed Wendell. He threw himself from bed and into his slippers and fussed around the nightstand for his spectacles.

"Dear Wendell," she moaned. "It's them riders!"

Wendell knew nothing about it and meant to demand explanations but the noise outside drove him to hysterics. Lightning spit and pissed down from the heavens and thunder with it, screams as long as the night ran in and out of every window and wall until Wendell found himself down on the floor along with her, him long without his bathrobe and baying about how he loved her and hoped and prayed this wasn't the last time for him to hold her.

"Them riders!" she cried. "They've come! We should never have moved here."

Wendell held her tight. Tales from childhood ran through his head but, never one for ghost stories, he dismissed them. But now...

He held her closer. Outside the wind howled and moaned and raised such a ruckus they reckoned more than just their house would be laid waste. Her shouts and cries mingled with the din and he figured he didn't want to hear them anyway, would rather just hold her. He fell over her and hoped it all to be quick.

And outside, all the while, hoof beats and wind whipping and men laughing. Men laughing.

"I love you, Rhonda," he said so many times it tasted like air. "I love you so much."

And an orange glow floated at the bottom corner of the window, then the bottom half, then it looked like all of outside had been colored bright orange and Rhonda shut her eyes tight until all she saw was black, but heard the crackling and snapping and couldn't be fooled into believing that everything was not afire outside the window.

Where men had once been laughing, she heard someone half-toning a church hymn or something like it, barely trying to keep in tune. "God is a-fore us, yes he is," he, whoever he was, kept singing. He had no other words to the song, just kept at that single lyric but kept at it proud. "God is a-fore us, yes he is, yes he is."

"I have to go out there," Wendell said. "Somebody could be in trouble."

She clutched him, and fingers like iron wouldn't loose him for nothing. He screamed for her fingernails. "You get yourself right back down here,

Wendell Penn," she cried. "Don't you leave me, do you understand?"

"There might be trouble in the neighborhood," he said. "Someone might need my help."

"Sit you back down here with me," she cried. "I need your help. Do you hear me? It's us! It's us they're after!"

And Wendell, having never heard fear tinge his wife's voice like so, forsook all other duty as extraneous and returned her back to his arms where she stayed until the orange glow at the window gave way to sun up and no more were the cracklings and snappings, but birds, birds carrying on outside. The branch from the old gum tree scraping across the roof's shingles due to a breeze. Wendell rolled off his woman and, for the first time, let her breathe.

He put a hand to Rhonda's shoulder and gave her a shake.

"We're dead," she moaned. "We're dead and I'm fine with it. I hate this street."

"We ain't dead," he said. He smiled and checked her for cuts and bruises and looked deep into her eyes to make sure everything was still ticking, then hefted himself to his knees and dusted his palms on the thighs of his long johns. He looked about the room and, using the nightstand for support, brought himself to his feet.

"You heard them horses last night, didn't you?" Rhonda asked from below.

"I don't know what I heard," said Wendell. "It sounded like a storm. I'm going to check the kitchen." He waved a hand in front of him as if surprised to see everything still intact, then made his way through the house. But each room—kitchen, living room, hallway—had been left to it and he found himself standing at the front door, jaw dropped down around his knees.

"You heard it well as I did," said Rhonda and he wondered how long she'd stood behind him. "It weren't no storm. It was horses. Men on horses. That's who made that noise."

"That weren't no horses, Rhonda," said Wendell. "Sounded more like a storm. A big one at that. I best head outside and check on the neighbors, make sure everybody's okay."

She rushed to him and grabbed his bathrobe by the belt. "No, Wendell. Don't go out there. Stay inside. If anything's wrong, somebody else will come and tend to it. It ain't our problem no how."

"Now, now," he said, holding her. "Everything's fine, baby. There ain't nothing to be afraid of no more. Storm's passed."

"No it ain't," she pleaded. "This storm ain't never going to be over. It started well before us and it'll keep blowing and blasting long after we're gone. There ain't never going to be an end to it and if there is, we'll be long dead. Please don't go out that door, Wendell. I know you heard me."

He tried to smile. He put both hands on her arm and softly moved her aside. "Honey," he said, "we need to check on our neighbors. They might not have been as lucky." She started to say more, but he didn't want to hear it. "It's our duty now." He stepped from her and opened the door.

Rhonda fell to a heap and choked on her own sobs. She didn't tell him because he was a good man. She knew Wendell would kick up a fuss if he caught wind of Wilbur Turgow and his ilk, hassling her and others like her. Wendell meant well, she figured, but he'd never accept their lot. He'd go out fighting and screaming and then where would she be? Where then?

She put her head in her arms and figured she'd rather suffocate herself with her own bathrobe than watch Wendell destroy himself when she heard him shouting. She poked up her head and listened to be certain.

"Rhonda," he hollered. "Rhonda honey, call the police!"

She leapt to her feet. Rather than track down the cordless, she raced outside. Wendell saw her coming and moved to tackle her, the entire time pointing and screaming and ordering her back inside.

"What's the matter?" she cried. "What is it, Wendell?" She doubted she could take much more. She lifted her eyes to the sky with full intention of asking what kind of God could allow this to continue for as long as it has when she saw it, raised up high in the shagbark hickory at the edge of her yard. Her mouth opened to scream, but nothing pushed forth. Faraway were chainsaws.

"Go back inside honey," said Wendell. He put his arms around her and blocked her view of the tree. "You don't need to see this."

She raised a crooked finger to the top of the hickory. "Wha—?"

"It's Mister Turgow," he whispered. "We'll need to call somebody to help get him down."

She put her head to his chest and he rushed his wife into the house, hoping to high heaven that she'd erase that and all other painful images from her mind. Hoping she could go on knowing nothing about what a terrible world in which they sometimes lived.

Long Gone Girls

Rose Yndigoyen

Dianna was always bothering Polly when she was trying to work—swooping down from the ceiling, begging for a kiss.

Polly shrugged and ducked. Dianna hit her shoulder like a moth bumping against a porch light, a blow that buzzed.

"You're no fun." Dianna flounced over to hover atop one of the tall filing cabinets. "Why don't you want to kiss me? I know you like girls. I heard you tell Thomas the other day that your girlfriend ignores you."

There were too many answers—you're a ghost, you're only seventeen, it scares me that I like it when you laugh—so Polly just ignored the question.

"I have to finish this."

She gestured at the dusty pile of photographs in front of her. She pulled another one off of the nearest stack, holding it carefully, her fingers only on the outside edges. She slid it into a clear plastic sleeve, slipped an identifying paper tag into its corresponding slot next to the picture.

Diver Descending into Lake Salvador. 1940. Board of Water.

The diver was halfway down a ladder, one foot tentatively stretched down toward the water's surface. His head was turned toward the camera, but his helmet was screwed on straight. From inside the helmet, one pale eye glimmered out at Polly, where the diver's ear should have been.

Polly liked the photo. She took out her phone, and tried to take a picture of it, but the poly sleeve made a glare. She slid the picture out again, and glided her thumb over the shutter button once, twice, three times until she had the strange, fixed stare exactly where she wanted it—in her hand.

She wasn't supposed to take pictures in the archive, but she did it almost every day. At home, in bed, at one or two or three am, she'd flick her phone on and make her own ghostly light, staring at the black and white boys and girls and bridges while Sara slept.

That was how Polly met Dianna, trying to find the right angle to capture the rage in the font of a BP protest poster. Dianna had inserted her hand into the frame and left Polly wondering whose fingers those were for a week before Dianna whispered in her ear.

"Mine."

And then that laugh, like wind chimes in a snow storm, tangled up in their own strings—eerie, not at all unpleasant.

Polly glanced up, but Dianna was still sulking, hardly visible.

Polly put the photo back into its sleeve, straightened the id tag, and laid it in a box marked with the appropriate year and collection.

The next Board of Water photo was boring—massive pipes and earth movers. Polly slid that pile away and picked up another photo, from a collection she loved more.

Eliza Ducout Field and unnamed escort, 1928, Estate of Eliza Ducout Field.

Eliza's pose in the picture was stiff, her right arm wrapped around a handsome boy, his left reaching around to squeeze her shoulder. But her smile has something more flexible in it.

Polly's eyes were drawn to Eliza's ear lobes. She had also seen pictures of Eliza as an old woman, ears stretched to drooping by heavy pendant earrings. She lingered on the picture of the teenaged girl, her earlobes still pert and whole.

Dianna never liked it when Polly mooned too long over long gone girls. It made her too mindful of her current state. She breezed by over Polly's head, stirring the air enough to disturb the pile of carefully penciled in identification slips at Polly's left hand.

Polly snatched for the papers, but a few drifted to the floor.

"Shit. Di—!"

Dianna giggled and Polly shivered a long, lovely shudder, just the same as if someone had run fingernails lightly up her bare arm.

"Hey. Lunch?"

Thomas didn't come all the way into the room, just poked his head in through the archive door. Dianna amused herself by pulling at his hair, but he didn't notice.

Polly nodded and put her pencil down. Dianna rolled it off the worktable and on to the floor. Polly left it there and Dianna frowned. Polly ignored her and grabbed her lunch bag. Dianna put a great deal of effort into it and kicked the pencil across the floor. Thomas watched the pencil roll, perplexed.

Polly followed Thomas into the hall, quickly closing the door behind her and tucking the keys into the pocket of her jeans. She figured now was as good a time as any for this conversation.

"I think this place is haunted."

He chuckled, but didn't answer, just steered them out back, to the small garden and café.

She tried again when they were in line for their coffee. The coffee served in the museum café was thin and sour, but an employee discount made it palatable.

"Really," Polly insisted. "Haunted."

"By who?" Thomas paid the cashier for both coffees and a soggy, saran wrapped sandwich for himself.

"A girl…" Polly didn't want to say Dianna's name.

Thomas raised his right eyebrow and slurped at his coffee while he waited for his change.

"I have proof." Polly insisted.

They settled in at their usual table, all the way in the corner. Polly lifted the top slice of bread from her sandwich and picked off half the turkey—Sara always gave her too much turkey.

Then she wiped her fingers on a napkin and toggled through a few menus on her phone, pulling up one of the pictures she had taken of Dianna.

"See?"

Thomas took a big bite of his sandwich before glancing at the screen.

"Right there…" Polly outlined Dianna's profile with her index finger.

"That's just…a…" It didn't really look like anything Thomas could think of, other than a nose and the pretty, pouting lips of a teenage girl. "…the flash. Or shadow. Or both."

A crumb fell from his lower lip to the upper right hand corner of the touch screen.

Polly flicked her napkin at the phone, dislodging the crumb.

"How could it be a shadow and a light at the same time?"

She knew what he meant though. Dianna was like that, clearest when she was a negative image of herself.

"Well, it's not a ghost. No such thing."

He took another swig of coffee, swallowed, burped into the back of his hand and changed the subject to the new cashier in the café.

"She's pretty cute right? Maybe I'll see if she…" Thomas talked on, his mouth full.

Polly stifled a gag, and put her sandwich down, smoothed the tinfoil around it and wrapped it back up, carefully overlapping the edges of the foil, as if she was wrapping a present. Sara hated it when she wasted food.

She paused before putting it back in her lunch bag.

If she forgot to eat it before she got home, Sara would grimace at the smell of spoiling mayo. Polly would mumble out something about Thomas chewing with his mouth open and Sara would wonder aloud whether "feeling sicked out" was a good enough reason for a grown woman to waste food. And then there'd be a lot of cold silence and no sex and a really elaborate lunch the next day and plenty of follow up questions about how everything tasted and if she'd shared any with Thomas, which she didn't feel like doing, especially not now that he'd started chewing with his mouth open.

Polly mashed her careful foil package into a ball and launched it toward the trash bin.

She made the shot.

Thomas scowled. "You're not always gonna get so lucky."

Rachel was passing, and disapproved. She veered her course toward Thomas and Polly.

"Pauline…"

Rachel was carrying her own cup of coffee—clearly not museum dreck, the cup was stamped with the logo of the organic café down the block. A thick froth of foam peeped over the top of the cup, dripping down over the marks that Rachel's lipstick had made on the rim.

"Polly." Polly corrected her.

"Riiiiggghht. That's cute. We should think of cute nicknames like that for the twins."

Polly watched Rachel mentally rearrange her nursery for a minute.

Polly slouched down in her chair while she waited, but thought better of it and sat up straight again, trying to keep a smile on her face. Rachel and Thomas were her only professional contacts at the moment, unless you counted Dianna.

Polly didn't count Dianna. Dianna was a decidedly unprofessional contact.

"…see me after lunch?"

Polly snapped back to attention.

"Sorry. Yes. Ok."

Rachel turned away. Thomas leaned across the table and whispered, "Told you."

"We haven't had much time to talk, Pauline." Rachel's eyes strayed to her computer screen as she talked. She clicked open an email, scanned it, clicked it shut again.

"It's Polly."

"You've been working upstairs. With the photos."

Polly nodded, "I've gotten through the first few boxes. The catalog is updated through about…"

Rachel waved a hand, dismissing the rest of Polly's sentence.

"As you know, our previous director left rather suddenly and I've been on leave…"

Polly took a deep breath and nodded, slowly.

"…but I've been sorting through some things and…"

Polly gnawed on her bottom lip.

"…I'm not quite sure how to say this, so I'll just get to the point. You don't actually work here, Pauline."

Rachel tilted her head toward Polly, waiting for an explanation.

Polly licked her lips. She didn't have anything in particular to say, so she stayed quiet.

"You've been showing up every day, working a full day, fraternizing with the staff, but no one hired you, no one advertised for an archivist, no one ever asked you to come in."

That wasn't exactly true. Dianna had asked her.

A month ago, Polly had gone wandering while Sara was in class. Used to cool coastal summers in New York, she had been surprised by the heaviness of the heat and thinking of turning for home when she felt a cool stream of air across her right cheek. It had made her turn her head toward the open museum door. She had walked in. The museum had been a grand house once. Now it was frayed and falling in on itself. But it was cooler than outside, so Polly stayed.

A chill at her back had sent her upstairs and through three gallery rooms—past a dusty scale model of the French Quarter, swampy looking landscape paintings and new color photos of Katrina and its aftermath.

Polly had taken a left at a photo of a refrigerator floating in a living room and found a door marched "Archive." The door had a lock but swung open when she pushed. She had settled herself at a table, looked through piles of photos for an hour, then put her head down and napped in the air conditioning for two.

Polly had awoken refreshed and sure she'd come back the next day. She paid admission on each of the next two days and walked straight to the Archive, bringing her own pencils. On the second night she lied to Sara—"I got a job."

She didn't pay admission again. Instead, Polly had waited in a corner until she could slip in to the staff offices behind Thomas, present herself to Marnie in HR and stumble over an explanation for her presence.

Marnie, a week away from retirement, had shrugged, handed her the archive keys, and said they'd sort it out when Rachel got back.

Two days later Polly took that picture of Dianna's hand. A week after that Dianna was greeting her good morning with a hug that made her teeth chatter.

Rachel was probably not interested in that explanation though. Her mouth was making the shape of the word 'go' and she was holding her hand out, expectantly.

"The keys. I need your keys."

"Now?"

"Excuse me?"

"I just…I left some things upstairs…" Polly's throat was closing; the words came out in a whisper, a wheeze.

The phone on Rachel's desk buzzed. She pursed her lips and looked Polly over again, squinting at her dusty fingertips.

"Well. Run up and bring them to me when you're done."

Polly nodded.

"Quickly. Now."

Polly closed the archive door, locked it from the inside and leaned against it, struggling to breathe. Dry heaves shook her body. Her eyes felt sandy and hot. She rubbed a hand across her face and tried to collect herself. This wasn't an entirely unexpected turn of events, after all.

Dianna floated down to hover at her left ear and tried to offer sympathy.

"She's a bitch."

"Stop using that word."

"Why?" Dianna blew a cool stream of breath across Polly's cheek and mouth.

"You never used it before I came."

"You don't know what I did before you came."

This was true. Dianna and Polly began in the middle. Polly thought it would be rude to pry, at first. And then they were well past introductions and she had never asked what had happened to Dianna, if it was gory or sad. She had never asked why she only saw her in the archive, even though she could hear things said far down the other end of the hall. She had never asked if she had been lonely before, or if she was ever scared, at night, alone.

This often happened to Polly when she met new people—given enough time, the decorum borne of her shyness hardened into shell-like curls of self-absorption.

Polly slowly buttoned her coat, from the bottom to the top. "Will you miss me?" she asked Dianna.

"You'll miss me more."

Polly watched from across the lobby. It was obvious that Rachel and Thomas were talking about her. Rachel scrunched up her nose in distaste and shrugged. Thomas laughed, and the word 'ghost' floated across the marble floor to Polly's ears.

She waited until Thomas had gone back into his office before she crossed the lobby to meet Rachel.

"Oh. Pauline."

Polly chewed the inside of her cheek to keep from correcting her.

"I brought the keys."

"You can leave them on the desk. And close the door behind you."

"Um…"

"Yes?"

"Maybe…I could…volunteer?"

Rachel shook her head, a slight smile on her face. "It's too late for that, now, isn't it?"

She walked off toward the conference room, the sound of her high heels half the speed of Polly's heart. Polly was alone, the keys dangling from her hand.

She stepped inside Rachel's office and positioned herself behind the half open door. She pulled her phone out and pressed redial.

"Sara?" Polly's voice was soft, not only because she was hiding.

"Hey. Babe. What's up? I can't talk…"

"I…I want to tell you something."

"I have *class* Polly. I can't…"

"Oh."

"Tonight though? I've got study group till late. But after, ok?"

"What?"

"Study group." Sara was clearly exasperated.

"Right. I forgot." Polly whispered.

"I have to get back." Sara said.

"Bye…love you."

Polly waited, but no response came. She slid her phone into her pocket. She missed the click you'd get from an analog phone, a noise that let you know for sure when you'd been hung up on, not merely mislaid.

She tucked herself further behind the door, dug out her own key ring and slid off two keys—the key for her bike lock, the key for the trash room in back of their building. She laid these on Rachel's desk and put the archive keys in her pocket.

The ladies room was humid; the small window that faced the garden had been open all day. Polly slid in through the window and then shut it, easing it down a half-inch at a time to be sure it didn't make a sound.

She entered a stall and sat on the back of the toilet tank, rested her feet on the closed seat lid. She took the keys out of her pocket and took a picture of them with her phone, her palm curled around them, the silver ring on her left ring finger a dull glint in the upper left corner of the photo.

Polly waited. Once security checked the doors and locked up, that was it for the night, nothing more elaborate was necessary for a small, moldering museum. There would be no alarm unless Polly tried to break a window or steal the one decent painting—another bayou landscape, but this one sharp and glowing, shot through with the rose gold light of a summer sunrise. It hung in the entrance hall, looming over the shabby desk where docents charged the very few patrons for entry.

Polly didn't want to steal it, but when everything had been quiet for an hour, she slipped out of the bathroom, took the long way around to the entry hall and stood in front of the painting for a minute to watch the water glow. The shifting moonlight through the window changed the brushstrokes from shining pink to silver gray and back again.

"Mine."

Polly felt icy fingers thread through hers, goosebumps ran up her wrist.

"I took the archive keys. I thought you couldn't come out here…"

"You don't know all the things I can do." Dianna whispered.

A flush rose to Polly's cheeks. She could feel the nervous rhythm of her heart jumping in her jugular vein.

Polly wasn't sure which way to turn, but she didn't need to move after all. Dianna met her mouth before she moved. Her kiss shone and shifted like the moon.

Visitin' Cormierville

Hardy Jones

We drove north out of Lake Charles and crossed a bayou with its cypress trees and stumps shrouded in wispy fog. After the bayou, rice fields began, signaling that we were close to the Cormier family house. At a small country store, we turned right and made our way a few miles back into the woods. This road was paved but it was old, narrow, and needed to be repaved. Instead it had been patched and repatched, making for a jarring ride.

Traveling to Grandmother Royal's penthouse was always dramatic and something I looked forward to, but the Cormier place was different. Mom and I had made a few summer trips here—Dad never came, saying he had to keep the nursery running—and the Louisiana heat and humidity was unbearable, especially since Grandma and Grandpa Cormier didn't have air-conditioning. At least this visit was in the fall, and the heat wouldn't be a problem. But mud, due to the rain, would be, because eventually we had to turn off this paved road and onto a dirt one. Relatives lived up and down the dirt road. In fact, all the people back in these woods were related, either by blood or marriage, to Mom and me, and due to this, the place's unofficial name was Cormierville. Even the dirt road was named after my Great-grandfather Homer Cormier, who, according to what Mom had told me, was the first white man to settle back here.

We turned left onto Homer Cormier Road and immediately the tires sank a few inches into the soft mud. We weren't stuck but the wheels threw mud that resounded deeply under the car. But Mom, driving like this was everyday fare for her, handled the car and muddy road with ease. My grandparents lived at the far end of the road, about a mile away, and when we made it to the halfway point, which was another road that diverted off farther into the woods and was named after one of my great-uncles, the road was no longer simply muddy, but under water. I wasn't sure we could get through and I didn't want to try it, but Mom, without hesitation, slowed down and headed into the murky quagmire. Rust-colored water spread in front of us and washed the car's undercarriage. Like a slow moving hydro-mobile, we rolled past the houses of aunts and uncles. A few hundred yards from my grandparents' house, the water receded and the mud again thudded under the car.

"Is Uncle R.J. going to be here?"

"No. He lives about ten minutes away, further up the paved road."

Mom parked the car in front of her parents' house on what seemed to be the highest and firmest point of land. Before we got out of the car, relatives, from toddlers to the elderly, slogged their way through the mud in knee-high rubber boots, and a crowd surrounded the car. At Grandmother Royal's, I was the prized grandchild, the final one of two grandsons; but here I was only one more grandchild lost in a list of two dozen. All the other grandchildren lived close by and had regular contact with Grandma and Grandpa Cormier, who never even called me by name.

The Cormier house was the antithesis of Grandmother Royal's penthouse. The house was single-story, wooden, weather-beaten gray with a sloping narrow front porch, and a rusty waist-high fence, drooping in front of the house. Grandmother Royal was tall, thin and stately; Grandma Cormier was short and rotund with thick arms and waist. Grandfather Royal was a shrewd businessman who died wealthy, Grandpa Cormier had worked in the logwoods, chopping wood for the local sawmill until he was too old to do it any longer and lived off a meager pension and Social Security benefits.

Five aunts and uncles, lips protruding with snuff, and a half-dozen muddy cousins who had funny accents met us at the car, not talking directly to us but murmuring to each other.

Grandpa, clad in faded overalls, the only clothing that I ever saw draped on his lanky body, stepped onto the front porch, a plastic coffee cup in his hand. He spit a thick brown juice onto the muddy ground and said: "What you doing here?"

"I've come to visit," Mom said.

"That husband ain't with you?"

"He's in Lake Charles resting. He drove us all night so we could be here this morning."

Mom stepped onto the porch and hugged her daddy; he wrapped one arm lightly around her in return. Mom went inside the house followed by the aunts and uncles. I wanted to follow too, but I didn't want to look

like a mama's boy in front of the male cousins who looked to be my age
and carried hunting knives on their belts which bore their names and
fancy buckles. Luckily, I was larger than any of the cousins there, and
after the excitement of our arrival, all but three, two boys and a girl,
went back to their homes.

"You're Wesley, ain't you?" the dark haired, bony girl with a swayback
said.

"Yeah."

"I'm Uncle Red's oldest girl. Name's Lois. You came here a few summers
back, didn't you?"

"Yeah."

"Is that all you say?"

"Maybe it's all he knows how to," one of the boys said, and took out his
knife, which had a six-inch blade, twirling it in his hand.

"I can say other things. I just don't feel like talking."

"You too good to talk to us because you're daddy's rich?" the boy said.

"No."

"Damn right you ain't."

I looked to Grandpa to see if he'd scold the boy for cursing, but he
seemed not to have heard; or maybe he just didn't care. Rules were
different in Cormierville.

I asked the boy holding the knife, "What's your name?"

"I'm blood kin and you don't know my name."

"That's why I asked."

Lois laughed at this. "He got you there, Coon."

"Coon? What type of name is that?"

"Mine. That's what type." He clenched the knife, which I noticed had
a serrated side.

"It's his nickname," Lois said. "We call him that because of the black
rings under his eyes. Grandpa says they look like a coon's mask on him.
Ain't that right, Grandpa?"

"You kids go play, but stay out of that mud." Grandpa crossed a long
leg over the other and spit again.

The only place to stay out of the mud was in the house, but I wasn't
venturing in there. Voices, some in French, some in English, but all loud,
met me outside. One minute there was laughter, the next the words and
voices sounded quarrelsome. I hoped Mom was ok.

The boys, who I took to be brothers by their similar builds and faces, walked across the muddy road and started throwing their knives in a big mud puddle. I was glad they walked away, even if it was only a few feet.

"Lois, do you have a nickname like Coon?"

"I'm the only Cormier who doesn't have a nickname. Even Coon's little brother there, he's called Hobo because he's always picking up cans and other trash from the side of the road and bringing it home and piling it by the back door."

"Hey, rich man's boy," Coon called.

"Don't call me that."

"Why not? Ain't your daddy rich?"

"No."

"That ain't what my daddy says. He says the only reason your mama married your daddy is because of his money."

"Well your daddy don't know shit," I said.

"Don't be talking about my daddy." Coon snatched his knife out of the mud puddle and pointed the blade toward me. "You think I could hit you from here if I threw this knife?"

"You probably could. But I wouldn't do it unless you want that knife shoved up your ass. Now what'd you call me for?"

Coon flipped the knife in his hand twice, then dried the blade on his jeans and slid it back into its sheath. "I want you to see something. Now come on over here."

I walked over and was glad that Lois accompanied me. Coon reached into his back pocket and I braced for another weapon. "You ever dip?" he asked, and produced a worn snuff can.

"I can't."

"Why not?" Coon asked, removing the can's lid. The smell was strong, like industrial strength nicotine laced mouthwash. Then Coon and Hobo filled their lower lips with it.

"It's against my religion."

"What kind of church don't believe in dipping?" Coon asked. "That sounds like a sissy church."

"It ain't. It's the Mormon Church."

"You can't be no Mormon," Coon said, "all Cormiers are Baptist or Catholic, except for Aunt Curly who married a Jehovah's Witness."

"My dad joined that church and Mom and I did too."

"That explains why Aunt Raynell don't dip," Lois said.

"Come on and take a little dip," Coon said, waving the can under my nose. "It won't hurt you."

"Don't listen to him, Wesley. I tried a dip once and was puking my guts out for the rest of the day," Lois said.

"That's because you're a girl," Coon said. "Now, Wesley, you're stronger than a girl, ain't you?"

"Of course I am, and that's why I'm not gonna try it."

"That don't make no sense," Coon said.

"There's more than just physical strength. There's the strength of belief. And taking a dip would go against my beliefs, so I'm gonna be strong enough to refuse."

"You sound like a preacher."

"I read a lot."

"That's a sissy thing to do," Coon said.

"It's better than throwing a perfectly good knife into muddy water."

"It's my knife and I'll do with it what I want. Maybe I'll use it to cut you."

"Maybe you will. Or maybe when you pull it I'll take it from you and cut you. And wouldn't you feel dumb then, getting cut with your own knife."

"You calling me dumb?"

"There's no need to state the obvious."

Coon reached for the knife and I tackled him to the cold, wet ground. Coon was stronger than I had expected, and he rolled me over once, covering me in mud, but I used my weight to get back on top and stuck Coon's head in the mud puddle. Hobo hit me in the back, and I turned and saw him pull his knife. I readied myself to jump off Coon and away from Hobo's blade, but before I had to Lois kicked Hobo in the knee, dropping him, and took his knife while he writhed on the ground.

I felt a hand lifting me and saw Grandpa, who held my arm above the elbow, pulling me up. Coon saw a chance for a surprise attack, but when he lunged at me, Grandpa knocked him back.

"What'd you attack Coon for?" Grandpa said.

"I didn't attack him."

"Don't lie to me, no. I seent you jump on him," Grandpa Cormier said, and spit in the puddle.

"He was about to stab me with his knife."

"It's true, Grandpa," Lois said.

Grandpa worked his tongue around his mouth, poking his lips out.

"You ain't got nothing to say, hahn, Coon? First time I ever hear you shut up. You must be guilty. I knowed your daddy shouldn't have bought you that knife. March yourself back to your daddy's house and don't come back down here today until you learn how to act." Coon and Hobo walked off, their rubber boots kicking up mud. "Now, you, you go inside to your mama."

"My name's Wesley, Grandpa."

Grandpa, oblivious to what I said, walked back to the porch and resumed his seat, crossing one leg over the other, and staring into the dreary day.

The Cormier house was as hot and smothering as it was in the summer. A wood burning stove sat in the center of the living room and inside it a fire popped and hissed. The wood floor was bare, and the furnishings were not extravagant: an old naugahyde recliner with duct tape holding the left arm together; a low cloth sofa the color of a smashed pumpkin was covered in oil stains; used coffee cans stuffed with paper towels were strategically located around the room, so no matter where you sat, you could spit into one of these crude cuspidors.

All the adults were in the kitchen. The aunts and uncles stood, leaning against the counters, while Mom and Grandma Cormier sat.

"Lost it all?" Mom said.

I stopped where no one could see me.

"Every acre," Grandma said in her heavily French accented English. "And he gone to Texas, got on at that rice mill."

"You shouldn't listen to grown folks' conversations," Lois said.

"That's how you find out things. Now step back so no one sees you and hush."

"Them children of his," Grandma said, "they broke him, yeah. Staying in trouble with the law and having children themselves and no man to support them."

"Who are they talking about?" I whispered to Lois.

"You tell me. This is how *you* find out things."

"That's terrible," Mom said. "I've got some distressing news of my own."

"You done left that loud-talking Texan?" Grandma asked, with hopeful glee in her voice.

"No."

"What you waitin' on, *chere*?" Grandma said.

"The time ain't right."

"Time ain't gonna get better, no. You not getting younger, and it hard for an old woman to find her a man."

Another man? That phrase slapped me in the face. That hadn't been part of the life I had dreamed of. It would just be Mom and me, and, for the first few months, until we got on our feet, Uncle R.J. and his family. But they would be temporary. In the end, it would only be Mom and me.

"My news involves Royal, though," Mom said.

"What that crazy man done did now?" Grandma asked.

While I barely knew Grandma, she was not endearing herself to me.

"He wants us to join the Mormon Church."

Murmurs shot through the aunts and uncles.

"Them folks what got more than one wife," Grandma said. "That don't sound good, no."

"They don't do that anymore. They're actually good people."

"*Mais ton pere* he was a deacon in the Baptist church," Grandma said. "How you gonna leave the Baptist church, *chere*?"

"The church doesn't get you into heaven. It's how you treat people that does. And, Mama, you were raised Catholic but converted to marry Daddy."

"*Vrai, mais* me I never stopped saying my rosaries."

"So I should convert but still be a Baptist at heart?"

"You shouldn't change churches at all," said an uncle with a potbelly. "That's just some more of that Texan wanting to change you. It's bad enough he took you away from us to live way in Florida. Now he wants you worshipping a different God."

"Mormons are Christian and worship the same God as Baptists and Catholics."

I felt good hearing Mom defend the faith.

"Me, I don't know any Mormons," an aunt with curlers in her hair said in a nasal-whine, "but I have heard they..."

"You shouldn't go by what you hear. If you don't know for certain yourself, then you shouldn't believe what you hear. People hear things about us Cajuns but don't know nothing for true, yet they believe what they hear as fact."

"Sound like you on that husband of yours side," Grandma said.

"I wasn't till I got here."

"What that mean?"

"It means I don't like the way all of you are talking bad about him."

"When has he ever deserved to be talked good about?" the potbelly uncle asked.

"Now. This very moment. For trying to get us to become Mormon."

"Why so for that?" Grandma asked.

"Because he's only doing it to keep us together. And that's despite catching hell from his mama and family about it. He's willing to suffer their ridicule for what he believes in, and he believes in us staying together even though he's caught me in the act of leaving him. Yet, he still wants me as his wife. Now, to my way of thinking, that's a good man, yeah."

Mom's family looked defeated and they all reached for the solace of their snuff.

"Boy, stop listening to grown folks' conversation," the aunt with the curlers said, "and come in this kitchen."

"What happened to you, son?"

"Him and Coon got into a fight," Lois said. "And Grandpa broke them up and sent Coon home."

"You all right, Son?"

"He jumped on Coon before Coon could pull his knife, and they rolled in the mud, but they're both ok," Lois said.

"Come give your Grandma a hug and a kiss," Mom said, "before we go."

From what I heard her say about Dad, Grandma didn't deserve a hug or a kiss. I stepped closer to this white-haired woman who spoke the funniest English I'd ever heard and saw tobacco juice, thick and brown, dribbling from her mouth. Disgusting. If she wanted a kiss, I decided she'd have to earn it.

"What's my name?"

"Your Raynell's boy, *cher*," Grandma said.

"That's true, but it's not my name."

"Son..."

"No, Mom. Grandma wants a kiss, but a grandma who doesn't know her grandson's name, doesn't deserve a kiss."

"That's his daddy in him," the potbelly uncle said.

"I bet you don't know my name either."

"But I know how to redden your backside."

"Burly, you're not touching my son."

"I forgot. No one can lay a finger on your boy. The son of a rich man and a mama who always wanted to be."

"I wanted good things in life," Mom said, "and I had enough ambition to leave these woods to get them."

"You was willing to marry a *fils de putain* and put up with his shit to get good things," Uncle Burly said. "All you is is a married whore."

"Burly, *dit pas ça!*" Grandma said. "*Ça c'est ton soeur.*"

"Was my sister. She stopped being a Cormier when she got married and left Louisiana and started looking down on all of us like we no count," Uncle Burly said.

"Let's go, Son."

"That's it," Uncle Burly said, "run back to your rich husband. Maybe he can make you forget us."

"I've never wanted to forget you," Mom said, "but the way you're acting, I'll gladly forget all of you." Tears poured down Mom's cheeks. "Except, you Mama. *J'va t'aime beaucoup toujours.*" Mom hugged her mama's thick neck, buried her face in her shoulder, and when Mom pulled back her face was crimson and her eyes watery, but the tears had stopped.

Only Lois followed us out, and that was good because she was the only one I liked and wanted to say a proper good-bye to. Mom told Grandpa good-bye, who still sat with his legs crossed unaware of the world beyond his coffee cup and snuff.

Mom went to the back of the station wagon and got a white sheet, which she used to set plants on to keep the potting soil from spilling on the car's upholstery when she made her watering rounds in Pensacola, and stretched it over the front seat so I wouldn't muddy it. Lois and I stood by the passenger door. "Thanks for keeping Hobo from stabbing me in the back. And this time I'll remember your name."

"That's good," she said, "but I don't know if you'll ever have a chance to say my name again."

"What do you mean?"

"I don't think you or Aunt Raynell will ever come back."

"We will. Despite what just happened, Mom misses her family a lot. She'll be back and, because of you, I'll make sure and come with her."

Lois smiled and I saw her overlapping top front teeth, which added character to her and made her, though I found it a bit strange to think this about a female cousin, pretty.

Mom tooted the horn as we pulled away and Grandpa Cormier sat stark still, not acknowledging our presence, but Lois, with her white rubber boots, bony legs, arms, and crooked teeth, smiled and waved until she was out of view in the car's mirrors.

Mom negotiated the muddy road in silence. Despite what I told Lois, I thought this truly may have been Mom's last visit to Cormierville. When we reached the blacktop, I said, "Are we going to see Uncle R.J. now?"

"We can't."

"Don't worry because you're upset."

"We can't go see him because he's gone," Mom said.

"What do you mean he's gone?"

"He lost his place and moved to Texas to get his old job back."

Now I knew that Uncle R.J. was the one they were talking about in the kitchen. He and Mom were the two most successful Cormiers, but now it was just Mom. I felt bad for Uncle R.J., but I looked at all of this as a sign from God.

Windblown

Kent Tankersley

He was right behind that tree. I stood perfectly still for a long minute, barely breathing, not daring to make a sound. Again it came, much closer this time, a flute-like song that poured from the woods beside the overgrown logging road I was standing in. I turned slowly, my binoculars ready. The bird, a Veery, was only a few feet away, but completely hidden in the underbrush, revealed only by a sound that could have come from another realm, an eerie melody that briefly penetrated the boundary between our world and someplace ethereal.

I had almost come to think of the Veery that way. After four summers of bird watching, I hadn't sighted the skittish songbird even once. A hundred times I'd heard them taunt me from their hiding places as I walked up some mountain trail, enjoying the same kind of solitude that the Veery itself seemed to insist on. A hundred times I strained to glimpse the reclusive singer, sometimes standing an hour waiting for it to recover from my approach and sing once again. After four summers I had begun to think of them as disembodied bird songs; lovely, but invisible, apparitions of the forest.

I'd been stalking this most recent apparition for some thirty minutes as I hiked along the road, following it deeper into a broad basin towards a large clearing that I had spotted in the morning from the ridge. Now I was almost upon him. A fern at the base of a tree dipped forward and I knew he was there, hidden only by the tree trunk between us.

I started to ease to my right when, out of the corner of my eye, I saw a movement and twisted around to see a man in the road only three feet away, staring hard at me. I'd been so focused on seeing the bird that I hadn't heard him come up. Immediately, I turned back to the bird, but knew he was gone. A bird like the Veery flees at the first sign of danger, the first hint that something's amiss. I faced the man.

"You sure as hell can sneak up on someone," I said, trying to control my anger.

He said nothing, this dirty, bearded stranger who looked at me with

vacant eyes. Feeling suddenly unsettled, I pulled the water bottle from my day pack and took a long drink while the man studied me without a word. I half-heartedly offered him some water. He looked tempted for a moment but then, as if remembering something important, shook his head no. Even that small wordless gesture made me feel uneasy. There was something so utterly quiet about him that he cast almost no presence despite his striking appearance. He reminded me of a hermit I had met once in the backcountry of the Smokies, a wild-eyed man who had let himself go completely feral. The man before me now seemed even wilder, so much a part of the forest, so "natural," that if he stood motionless before a tree you might not even see him. His hair was long and windblown, twisted into tangled strands. His beard hung like a matted bib below the creased, weathered skin of his expressionless face. His eyes seemed half-glazed over, and I noticed he held his head tilted ever so slightly to one side, as if listening for something in the woods behind him, perhaps something no one else could hear.

Although it hadn't rained since morning and it was warming up here in the sheltered basin, he wore a heavy trench coat, like something from a World War I movie, a faded, mud-spattered garment far too big for him, revealing only his head and his old-fashioned high-top leather boots. His hands—I could imagine those with long, untended fingernails—didn't reach beyond the sleeves.

Finally, he broke his silence with a raw voice. "Where am I?"

"What?" I snapped, slinging my pack on. He didn't answer right away. "Don't you know where you are?"

He watched me with a face as blank as a rock that held no warmth of its own.

"How did you get in here?" I asked. "Did you come from the valley? Or the parking lot? Up on the ridge?"

That seemed to register something in him.

"Then you're going in the right direction. On up this road. It's three or four miles." As I pointed, his eyes seemed to follow my outstretched arm past my fingertip to where the road disappeared around a bend. He looked back to me, his head seeming to tilt even more from the strain of human conversation and, without another word, walked away.

I watched him for a moment before I turned to continue on my own way, glad to put some distance between us. Obviously strung out, I decided, on God knows what. Or maybe a genuine lunatic, some sort of escapee hiding up here in the mountains, easily homicidal. When that crossed my mind, I looked back over my shoulder. He was gone—the road was empty.

Where could he have gone? I wondered. I was sure he hadn't had time to reach the bend in the road. Had he ducked into the woods to follow me? I shook my head to dismiss the notion; he didn't seem lucid enough to be that crafty. Still, I decided it was best to keep my eyes open. As I continued down the road, I didn't quicken my pace, but neither did I stop to investigate any birds.

An hour later, as I entered the wide clearing, the site of a logging camp during the Depression, my uneasiness had vanished almost as if I had never seen the strange man. I paused to watch a cooperative warbler as it flitted from bush to bush, fleeing, and then returning—like a deer—alarmed but irresistibly curious about me. If any Veeries were around, they were keeping quiet, watching from under the moist shadows of some Rhododendron.

From the clearing I had an unobstructed view of the mountains looming over the basin. These were strange mountains for North Carolina, not the normal ridges and peaks smothered in dense forest. Here the upper slopes were covered only in grass and brush, their contours completely open to view. Seventy years before, wildfires and lumbermen had left only broad swaths of bare ground across these high peaks. Trees eventually returned to the more sheltered spots, like this basin. But the ridges, exposed to the mile-high winter winds, never recovered and could nurture only hardy grass and small scrubs. From a distance, the open slopes looked like manicured grounds, scattered here and there with bleached-white tree stumps. It was the strange beauty of this forsaken landscape that brought me here time and again to be immersed in the place. Looking up at the ridge, I could see I wasn't the only one.

On the crest high above, I could make out a long procession of weekend hikers, distant figures in bright red and orange, moving in single file along the exposed spine of the mountain. What a crowd up there! Each hiker was briefly silhouetted as they crossed the highest summit, then dropped out of sight, almost as if caught off guard by the wind and sent flying into the vegetation-choked gorges to the south. The wind keeps these—her captive peaks—swept clean, I thought.

Just as well that I chose to explore a much more secluded spot. The clearing was larger than it appeared from high on the ridge. This must have been the main yard of the logging camp, where the logs were loaded onto a narrow-gauge train that crept down to the settlements once a day with heavy loads of raw timber. My grandfather had been a cook in such a camp in Tennessee forty years before my birth. From his stories of that time, I could almost picture the empty clearing as it would have been back then, booming with relentless activity, but perhaps no less lonely a place. In its heyday, this peaceful grassy space would have been a plot of muddy ground surrounded by rough barracks, machine sheds and mountains of felled trees stacked beside the tracks.

During the day, only yardmen would have been working here, man-handling the timber dragged in by mule teams, and listening for the whistle of the engine pulling up from the valley. At night, the loggers—tough, sullen men—would return, filling the camp. Many were desperate farmers like my grandfather, forced by the Depression to sell their worthless farms, or drifters looking for enough money to drift a little further, or even criminals on the lam, hiding here on the edge of society.

As I poked around at half-buried pieces of rusting metal, I recalled that my grandfather often spoke of how unhappy these camps could be: too many men and too much work, boredom and despair. At first there had been hunting to fill their rare free-time, but soon they had shot most of the game there was to shoot. Only the company ban on liquor kept them from shooting each other. And they certainly found no inspiration in the beauty of the mountains they were paid to strip bare. Each one must have longed for the day he could go home and escape the place. Perhaps a few never did. My grandfather had laid his younger brother—crushed by a runaway log—to rest in the tiny graveyard that served his camp. Perhaps, here too in this clearing, men remained buried in the ground somewhere nearby, abandoned even by the memory of anyone who would have ever known they existed.

I had expected to find someone camped out down here, but the place was deserted, with no sign of any visitors except a campfire ring at the base of a tall balsam standing alone in the center of the clearing. I decided it was the perfect spot to eat some lunch and maybe take a nap before returning to the car by the more direct route up through the steep meadows.

It was surprisingly breezy in such a sheltered basin. Wind hissed through the solitary tree, swinging a pair of worn-out black boots that hung beneath its boughs, apparently left behind by some hiker. A peculiar ornament on a forgotten Christmas tree. The boots troubled me, looking—as they did, with some imagination—like the shoes of someone hanging within the green boughs of the balsam. Knowing that people can come to such beautiful, isolated spots also for the unhappiest of reasons, I parted the branches of the tree to be certain that nothing else hung there. I was relieved to see that indeed only the boots, weathered and beaten and draped over a limb by their laces, hung there. I felt foolish for thinking otherwise.

I sat beside the fire ring to work on my lunch of trail mix and jerky, and had no reason to give the boots another thought. Or shouldn't have. Occasionally, as I gazed at the mountains surrounding my clearing, the wind would sling the soles together in a loud thump that startled me. With the wind teasing the sheets of my notebook, I listed the morning's bird sightings, which weren't really that many. Again, I was reminded of how close I had come to seeing the Veery.

Finishing off my trail mix, I lay on the ground to watch clouds scuttle across the sky above the tree towering next to me. In the warm sun, I let myself drift off to sleep, but the boots knocking around in the breeze kept waking me. I was becoming more and more irritated by their jarring presence. Finally I was able to doze off completely, only to be roused from an unsettling dream by the loud groan of a tree limb under a sudden gust of wind and the boots violently thrashing about. I sat bolt upright, dazed for a moment, with the dream's image of vacant, watchful eyes lingering in my mind. I decided it was time to go.

Though the afternoon was getting on, there was no reason to hurry. The car was only about two hours away through the meadows, still close enough for me to take my time and enjoy the stark beauty of the place a little longer. The trail up the open slope wove in and out of scattered thickets of stunted birch, which from below in the clearing had appeared only as low scrubs.

I was half-way to the parking lot when a bird, flitting into a trailside bush, brought me to a stop. I stood quietly, waiting patiently to see if he would show himself. Then, from behind me I noticed a thumping noise, strangely familiar, floating up from below. Curious, I turned to scan the basin for the source of the rhythmic sound. Even at such a distance I could tell it was coming from the old logging camp I had abandoned just an hour before. Of course, I thought, the boots. But there was something more, something I didn't understand.

I trained my binoculars on the clearing, and located the lone balsam, now far below me. I pulled the tree into sharper focus, and for a second was merely baffled by the trench-coated figure of a man in its windblown boughs turning, slowly turning, at the end of a taut rope.

And then he was gone.

The
Confession

Miranda Stone

want to know which of you did it." Pa held out his wallet, opening it up to show it was empty. "I had a damn five in here. Who took it?" He pushed the grimy cap back from his forehead to peer at them.

Caleb focused his stare on the battered wallet. He made a point of studying its frayed edges and ignoring the way his brother Billy squirmed next to him. Out of the corner of his eye, Caleb didn't see his sister moving at all. Lena knew better than to draw attention to herself.

"All I raised is a bunch of goddamn thieves," Pa went on, shaking his head. "If your mama was alive, she'd turn your asses out. Now I'm givin' you one last warnin'. Someone had better fess up."

Caleb shifted his weight from one foot to the other, clasping his hands behind his back so tightly he cut off the circulation to his fingertips. The floorboards groaned beneath his sneakers. As he held his breath, feeling beads of sweat pop out on the bridge of his nose, he thought of his mother and how she used to sprinkle baby powder on the wooden floors. "Stops the creaking," she said with a wink. Now even that small trace of her was gone from the house. The floors were noisier than ever.

Before anyone could cave in, Pa reached forward and snatched Lena by the arm, drawing her to him. She let out a holler of surprise and then fell quiet. Caleb exchanged a quick glance with his brother.

"Take off your shirt, girl," Pa said. He began unbuckling his belt.

"Pa," Billy said.

"You gonna admit to doin' it?" Pa asked, his voice booming. Billy gnawed on his lower lip and didn't answer. Pa turned back to Lena. "Take it off."

Lena looked from Caleb to Billy, her eyes filled with pleading as she clutched the top button of her blouse with both hands.

"Take it off, or I'll rip it off your back." Pa held the belt now, his hands wringing the worn leather.

Lena turned her back on them, unbuttoned the shirt, and let it fall to the floor. She folded her arms over her bare breasts and waited, tremors coursing through her skinny frame. Pa let her stand there for a long time, never giving her any warning when she could expect the first strike. He hit her hard, and the belt buckle bit into her flesh. Livid welts rose before he could throw the belt back for another aim. Lena whimpered. A couple of times she stumbled forward but quickly righted herself so Pa wouldn't have a reason to grab her.

By the fourth slap of the belt against her skin, she was wailing. The sound filled the two-room shack and made the hunting dogs outside begin to howl. Billy turned to Caleb and shoved him. "Tell him you did it, goddamn it!"

Pa froze mid-strike. The belt fell limp at his side. Caleb swallowed hard and stared at Lena's back, praying the marks wouldn't leave scars. "You ready to talk?" Pa asked him.

Caleb stepped forward and cleared his throat so his voice wouldn't grate. "I did it," he said. "I took the money to buy me some cigarettes."

"Come here," Pa said. "I'm just gettin' warmed up."

Lena ran for the safety of the back room. Caleb took her place, stripping off his shirt and waiting for the first blow.

Half an hour later Caleb sat on the porch. He'd never bothered to put his shirt back on; cotton fibers felt as scratchy as burlap against those welts. Pa had left for the bar in his pickup, and Billy was long gone—he'd hightailed it out of the yard as soon as Caleb's beating started. Neither of them would be home for hours. Caleb scratched the oldest hound behind the ears and took a drag from a cigarette.

The shack door opened, and Lena came out to sit on the step beside him. She'd changed into a slip that should have been consigned to rags long ago. The straps slid off her shoulders. A balmy spring breeze stirred the trees in the yard, caressing Caleb's back like gentle fingers.

For several minutes they didn't speak. Caleb passed the cigarette to Lena, and she brought it to her lips. "Why'd you take the money?" he finally asked.

She narrowed her eyes in the haze of the smoke. "I had to get some female things," she said. "I was meanin' to tell him, Caleb." She handed the cigarette back to him.

"Wouldn't have done no good to tell him, and you know it. Next time you're needin' some money, you come to me. You hear?" He looked over at his sister. Lena avoided his stare but nodded. She didn't ask him how he would earn the money. Whenever Caleb came home with a few extra

dollars in his pocket to give her, Lena raised her eyebrows in a question, but Caleb never explained. Some things even a sister shouldn't know.

Lena climbed to her feet and tousled Caleb's hair. "Come on in and let me see if I can find somethin' to put on your back," she said. She squatted on her haunches behind him and draped her arms loosely around his neck. He could feel the threadbare fabric of her slip and her small breasts beneath it. "Goddamn, he sure got you good."

"Always does," Caleb said with a bitter grin. He ground out the cigarette and followed Lena inside. She propped the door open to let in the evening breeze, and as Caleb stood in the front room and watched her move through the shadows, a gust of wind stirred the stale air of the shack. He took a deep breath and caught a scent, raising his head like one of the hounds. The odor was faint but unmistakable, flooding him with memories of dark hair and smiling eyes. Baby powder.

Canaan

Caitlin Cauley

Does it go...?"

"There? Of course it does."

She blushes and looks to the side. "Sorry. I forgot it's not your first."

A rakish smile spreads across his lips. "But it's yours?"

She punches him lightly on the arm. "Of course it is, you idiot."

Outside the sun is beating down full upon the earth. It's far too hot to be anywhere but in the shelter of the farmhouse. There's no wind to rustle the yellowing tobacco leaves. The season has been hot and dry. The season before wasn't much better. The air is shimmering, weighted down in the wet heat of a rain that's promised for months but never comes.

"Right there?"

"Yes." Her eyes are half-lidded and her mouth hangs slightly open, her brows starting to furrow. The closer he comes, the deeper the lines on her forehead. "Right...right there."

The whole of the house is silent, everyone else gone for the day to town. She's supposed to be sick, and he's supposed to be watching the animals.

She grips his freckled shoulders. An involuntary cry slips out. They match breaths, their sandy hair flops in the same wave, their green eyes lose focus. Everything matches. All is the same. She feels everything, and then she feels nothing.

The congregation has gathered for a special prayer meeting, lifting up their voices for rain. The town is dying as fast as the crops. They've all massed together in the clapboard building with the windows and doors hanging wide open. The ladies hold fans. The men mop their brows. Nothing can stop the sweating and the sticking and the smell that rises and hovers above their heads.

"And Moses said unto them, in Exodus, my children, Moses said...Why chide ye with me? Wherefore do ye tempt the Lord?" The preacher's sleeves are rolled up and his shirt is sticking to his chest. His potbelly strains against the now-translucent white cotton. His wife tried to make him cut down on buttering his biscuits when he popped a button straight into a parishioner's eye one Sunday last September.

"And he struck that rock! He struck it and by the grace of God water poured out!" The preacher pounds his fist on the pulpit before he starts pacing. "My children, there are none of us who believe. We do not believe and how does our God punish us?" His voiced catches in a practiced choke and he shakes his fists at the sky. "We need to believe, children! We need to believe, and just being here in this church is not enough!"

Her fervor has robbed him of breath. He bends over, hands on knees, sweat dripping from the tip of his nose. He looks up and sees the raptured face of one of the teenagers. He can't remember her name to save his life. This one's face is glowing, from sweat and from faith, and her hands are stretched as high as they can go. Her twin brother is still sitting, doubled over, hands clasped. The preacher can see it in his mind's eye, limbs caught together, tumbling sun-streaked hair. He stumbles back to the pulpit and leans upon it to hide his pants which were straining now as much as the buttons on his shirt.

He ducks behind the building after the service, pretending at a migraine to avoid pressing the flesh as the congregation flows out the front door. He rolls a cigarette and strikes a match and tugs at his sweat-soaked shirt. His heart finally slows down a few beats with the first puff.

"Thank you, preacher."

He snaps to attention to see the girl, the sandy-haired female half of the pair from the front row. Her faded floral cotton sundress is clinging to the curve of her breasts and hips, and he can see the damned picture in his head again. "Thank you, young lady. God bless you."

She looks down with a bashful cast to her face. "I hope it does rain. I don't see how it can't."

"God's will be done, sweetheart."

"My mama wants you and the missus to come to the house for dinner this afternoon." Her eyes twitch upward and the preacher is lost in the clear green for a moment.

"Why...why of course."

She claps her hands and bounces on the balls of her feet. "I'll go tell

mama that we'll be setting out two more places." She turns and runs and he stares at the flying hemline of her dress and her long, lithe legs.

"Thank you for this delicious meal, Mrs. Brown." The preacher leans back and makes a show of patting his corpulent belly. His wife purses her lips, waiting for another button to pop and smack the gracious hostess right on the forehead.

"No, Pastor Mitchell, thank you for gracing us." Mrs. Brown reaches out to pat her husband on the hand and smiles at their two children.

"Yes, thank you," says the daughter. Her eyes are still shining like they did during the sermon. Everyone is oblivious to the venomous stare Mrs. Mitchell shoots her way. "I promise, we'll believe and we'll pray and it'll rain. I know God will grant it." She can't stop staring at the preacher, and Mrs. Mitchell's lips purse even further than thought possible.

"Like I said already, God's will be done, Angie." Pastor Mitchell sips from his nearly-empty lemonade glass. "I will say, it's wonderful to see young people like you and Bobby so devoted to the Lord."

Mrs. Mitchell twists her hands beneath the table. She takes a deep breath and tries to plaster a smile on her face. The resulting effect is like to a badger and she knows that someone at the table will notice eventually. "Excuse me, I need to step out for a minute." She abruptly pushes back from the table and lets the screen door bang behind her on the way to the porch.

She sits down in a rocking chair and presses a hand to her forehead before the dizziness gets to her. "And that ye defile not yourselves therein," she mutters. She'd seen how Bobby rested his hand on the small of his sister's back. She'd seen Angie's face during the service from her seat in the choir loft. She feels the bile rise up in her throat.

The rain comes in August. The clouds roll across the sky and the whole town holds its breath. Pregnant with expectation and waiting, the air hangs still. Angie stands out in the yard, watching her brother and her father walk up and down the tobacco field. She thinks that the first drop is just her imagination, and the second one too. The third, fourth, and fifth snap her into sharp reality. She looks up and tries to count the raindrops and she stretches her arms out. A grin spreads across her face.

"Hallelujah!"

She is struck with an idea and begins running down the road toward the church. The rain follows her and soaks her through to the bone. Her hair is sticking to her scalp and dripping into her eyes but she knows the way by memory. Behind the church is the modest parsonage and she bangs breathlessly on the door.

Pastor Mitchell answers and his face blanches.

Angie wheezes. "It's raining, preacher! Like you said! I prayed and Bobby prayed and Mama and Daddy prayed and it's here!" She beams. The preacher can only see the rivulets of water tracing from Angie's face to her neck to the rising curve of her chest.

"Come in, sweetheart." He opens the door wider and ushers the girl in. "Mrs. Mitchell is gone to visit her mother in the next county, but there should be something dry of hers you can wear." He casts a guilty look at the open Bible on the kitchen table. It is Saturday and he has no sermon prepared.

"Thank you, thank you so much." Angie looks down at her own soaked shirt and slowly reddens. She bites her lower lip and casts her eyes over to the side as Pastor Mitchell ushers her to the bedroom and shuts the door behind her. He begins to pace.

Another knock sounds from the front door. The preacher hesitates in the kitchen and pulls the frayed ribbon bookmark into the Bible before shutting it. He opens the door.

"Pastor Mitchell, is Angie here?"

The preacher feels like his collar is suffocating him and he fumbles with the top button to pull it loose. "Bobby. She's putting on something dry."

Angie's twin steps inside. "Reckon we both ought to wait the storm out here. Daddy just wanted me to go find her. She never just runs off like that."

"Go…go find something dry to put on for yourself." Pastor Mitchell waves Bobby away toward the bedroom and sits down in an armchair in the den and closes his eyes. He tries to breathe deep and feels like his heart is going to beat out of his chest. He tries to remember what he'd been reading before Angie showed up on the doorstep.

He picks up the shut book from the kitchen table and clutches the worn brown leather tight. He can feel a burn creep up the back of his neck. The bedroom door opens and he hastily tucks the Bible away into the cabinet below the sink before returning to the den. He sits down in the armchair, across from the twins, who are now clasping hands on the couch and whispering.

"My children, I know we're not papists, but is there anything you might want to tell me to get right with the Lord?"

The rain pounds on the shingled roof and the three sit in silence. Pastor Mitchell stands up and moves to sit in between the twins. They sit for a while longer before the preacher puts a hand on each twin's thigh.

"And know, my children, these sins against the Lord!" Pastor Mitchell is pacing behind the pulpit again. He looks at his wife in the front row and feels a stab of pain in his chest. He kneels down.

"We can only...we can only kneel before Him!" The preacher clutches at his chest again with each stab of fiery pain. He does not even dare look past the front row. The Brown twins are absent for the seventh week in a row, even as their parents sit in the back pew with sallow, sunken faces.

Mrs. Mitchell's face is serene. She watches her husband as his breathing becomes labored and he continues to kneel before his Lord and everyone else. She has seen the Brown girl and her husband has not. The girl was retching behind the general store last Thursday afternoon and Mrs. Mitchell knew. She knew.

"We...we kneel..." The preacher's breath catches. His face has become redder and redder with each breath and now he crumples.

The congregation watches. They wait for this fit of the Spirit to pass. They wait for an eternity for the preacher to come back up.

The night falls sooner with every passing week. Angie lies on her bed. She hasn't left for months. She looks out the window, looking for stars or a moon behind the rain clouds that have stayed for an eternity now, drowning out the last of her father's farm. She prays for Bobby, who left one night a month ago and hasn't returned.

Angie cries out. She rolls over on her side and clutches at her swollen belly with one hand as the other one twists in the sheets until her knuckles have turned white. She wails. Her parents do not come from their room, where they have been shutting themselves away every night since Bobby left.

Angie feels a trickle of warmth on her sheet. She curls up and her wails fade to a whimper and her moss-green eyes, once bright and clear, squeeze shut.

Tuesday Night Chorus

Heather Bell Adams

My mother's friends drove up in their SUVs and parked all along the driveway in front of our house. Now some of their tires are pushed up against the decorative rocks that line the yard. Our house, like most of the other houses on the street, is very large and very brown. The women got out of their cars and came into the house without ringing the doorbell. They have sleek, straight hair and shiny lips and big bracelets. Cashmere capes and smooth foreheads and dark red short nails. I don't know if they are here for garden club or bridge group or a wedding shower or a divorce party.

When I go out onto the second floor landing, I can see them downstairs in the kitchen. Most of them are drinking red wine. A few have coffee mugs or glasses of water. No one seems to be eating the cookies sprinkled with powdered sugar that are arranged in short stacks on silver trays. When I was younger, I would crouch down on the landing and spy on my parents and their friends below, my fingers wrapped around the iron railings that looked like ropes. Now that I'm in high school, I realize that I can see and hear just as much by walking across the landing as though I am going to the linen closet, which is down the hall, and then back again after a few seconds. Nobody even looks upstairs anyway. They are talking and laughing.

"You're never going to believe this, Cathy. That new family, the one that moved in down the street from us last week? Tommy heard they paid all cash."

"You're kidding me. All cash for that house?"

"I know," the first woman says. She nods and raises her eyebrows. Other women are talking about what Ginger Byrd was wearing at the Save-a-Child fundraiser—something way too short and tight for someone her age. Another woman asks, "Did you hear that Justin got a golf scholarship? And somebody else says, "It's a shame about Meredith Scarsdale, bless her heart. Still, she ought to have known better than to go to a stylist nobody's ever heard of."

I don't care about any of the things they're saying. I keep listening to be sure, but there isn't anything good. They don't mention Judith. Why would they? Even though she goes to my school, Judith doesn't live in this neighborhood. She lives with her mother over on the other side of Macon and they barely have enough money to keep the heat on in the winter. Judith's sister is a sophomore and a year older than we are, but it's not like she's popular or anything. There's no reason for any of these women to mention either of those girls.

When it gets close to six thirty, I lean over the railing and try to get my mother's attention. We need to leave by six forty to make it on time. A few of the women have left, but others are still standing around. My mother sees me and she tilts her head like she doesn't understand what I'm trying to tell her. Doesn't she remember that it's Tuesday?

After a few more minutes, I go to the bathroom to brush my hair. My jeans are slipping down and I find a white scarf that I loop through the belt loops and tie in a bow. I grab my boots from the closet and head downstairs.

Everyone looks up when I appear in the kitchen. "Look at you," they say, and "How old are you now, Alexis?"

"What a skinny thing you are!"

"Do you have a boyfriend, sweetie?"

"I hear you're going to be a cheerleader. How exciting!"

I mostly ignore them because I don't really know what to say. My mother is standing by the espresso machine. Her silk sweater matches the purple orchid on the kitchen island.

"Mom, we've gotta go."

"Go where, sweetie? Come try one of these darling cookies." She speaks in a loud voice and everyone stops their conversation to listen to us.

"It's Tuesday. I've got, you know. Chorus?"

She stares at me blankly and then slaps her forehead. Her bracelets jingle on her arm. "That's right. Everyone, I've gotta take Alexis to chorus, but I'll be back in a few."

One of the women asks what chorus. "I thought the school chorus didn't have tryouts until the spring," she says. "For freshmen anyway." She has big diamond hoop earrings and is holding a glass of iced water with a slice of lemon floating in it.

My mother laughs. "Not school chorus." She shakes her head. "Have you heard Alexis sing? She's way past that. No offense."

"Oh, no offense taken," the woman says and my mother has her leather tote bag hooked over her arm and her car keys in her hand.

On the drive, she tells me that I didn't need to hiss at her in the kitchen. A simple reminder would have sufficed. And the least I could've done was speak nicely to her friends. They are important women and I am old enough to carry on a conversation like a lady. She talks about impressions and respect and appearances and standing up straight.

"Why'd you tell them about cheerleading?" I ask. "When you know I didn't make it?"

"Because you're trying again in the spring, aren't you?"

"I don't think so. I don't really want to."

"Of course you are. I've reserved the activity center in the neighborhood. Once it gets closer to tryouts, you and your friends can practice there after you finish your homework. Okay? Get the kinks out?"

"Fine," I tell her. "Whatever." No matter what I say, she will make me practice. She'll ask why I can't manage to get in position at the right time and she'll say that I need to smile bigger. She'll tell my father that I'm lazy and should have my cell phone taken away unless and until I make the squad. All I do is text boys anyway and what's the point because I still don't have a boyfriend. Every one of her friends' daughters has a boyfriend and she doesn't know what my problem is. That's what she will say.

We pull up and I open the car door as soon as she stops the car. She bends her head to see me through the window. "Be back in an hour to pick you up."

"Okay." I close the door and walk down the gravel driveway. The house is smaller than ours and there is more color. The front door is bright yellow and red flowers are planted in big clay pots on the porch. The glass side door that I use is on the right side of the house. It's unlocked and I walk in and go down the hallway, where there is a navy blue rug with tiny white flowers along the edges. At the end of the hallway, I go up the small staircase to get to the bonus room above the garage.

Dr. Tanner stands up when she sees me. She's wearing a thick black headband in her grey hair and a white sweater with a long gold necklace and light blue pants.

"Alexis, it's so good to see you. Come, have a seat." She sits down in her chair and I sit on the white couch across from her. There's a pillow beside me, and Dr. Tanner nods when I put it in my lap. I look down at the gold fireflies on the dark pink fabric.

"Last week," she says looking in a green notebook, "you got very upset. You were crying." She looks up at me. "You say you don't know what those boys did to Judith. Is that right?"

I shrug. I act like my mind is blank, but I remember being there under the bleachers. I can picture it like I'm standing there right now. There was dirt and crunched up soda cans and Banks Murphy, who said he could get me invited to the party where the juniors would be. Evan, my one good chance at a boyfriend, was going to be at the party. Judith with her stupid, stupid big chest was standing there beside me like some kind of an idiot, waiting for me to tell her what to do. Judith, who acted like I was her friend. But come on, she helped me sometimes with my homework. That was it.

"You came. Alright," Banks said, taking his phone out of his pocket and typing a text.

"Yeah, so about Saturday—Evan's coming too, right?" I asked.

"Um, yeah, I think so. Probably."

I turned around to leave and Judith started to follow me. Banks stepped forward like he was going to stop her. I looked at him and he made a sort of squeezing motion with his hand.

"No big deal, Alexis. Seriously," he said. "Just be cool."

I tell Dr. Tanner that I didn't know what was going to happen to Judith. Not really.

"I think it's something we need to explore further. The extent of your knowledge, I mean," Dr. Tanner says and she waits for me to say something. I sigh. I've told her all this already. He texted me to bring Judith right then, before lunch period ended, and he said Evan would be at the party that weekend. That he could get me invited. And I don't know. Maybe those boys, Banks and the others, wanted to touch Judith like that.

"She didn't have to come with me. She didn't even ask me what we were doing. She's so stupid sometimes. She just stood there. He told me there was nothing to worry about. That's what he said. And then he told me to leave and that he'd see me at the party. Leave her there, that's what he meant." I wait for Dr. Tanner's response, asking myself why Judith didn't run away. She could have. It's not my fault she didn't.

Dr. Tanner writes something down in her green notebook and then looks up at me. "And what about the next day at school? Did you talk to her? Find out if she was okay?"

"She was there, but she was different. She had cut her hair and dyed it brown and there was something else that looked different about her too. It wasn't only her hair. I don't know what it was."

"And did you talk to her?" Dr. Tanner asks again, even though I heard that question the first time.

Judith didn't talk to me. She hasn't talked to me since then. "She'll never talk to me again." I tell Dr. Tanner and I shrug, like I don't really care.

"You don't know that. You don't know never again," Dr. Tanner says and she shakes her head.

She has asked me every week, for three weeks now, why I'm having such trouble eating. I don't answer her. I don't want to talk about it. Every week she waits for me to answer and I don't say anything. She asks me again tonight.

"Do you see food as the enemy, Alexis? Do you feel that you want to disappear?"

I shrug again and then, for some reason, I remember my mother lying to her friends about how I'm such an amazing singer. "You know what? I'm really not a very good singer at all."

Dr. Tanner raises her eyebrows. "I'm afraid I'm a little lost. I'm not sure where the conversation is going, but I'll wait for you to explain." She puts down the green notebook and leans forward. I squeeze the pillow on my lap and decide it's time to tell her.

I was at home that night, the day that I'd taken Judith to the bleachers—when I left her there after lunch. It was dinner time and we were sitting at the dining room table. There were thick white dishes and gray cloth napkins and the big chandelier above us with its rows and rows of candle-shaped lights. My parents were both staring at me, like they always do. My father spooned out mashed potatoes and plopped them onto his plate—two big, white lumps of them. All I could see was Judith and her big breasts. I looked away and stared at the rolls in their woven basket safely wrapped in a soft cloth napkin.

How many hours had it been since Judith and I had lunch together? Six? When she ate by herself, she went over to the band building. But I told her that was lame. On the days that we ate lunch together, we always went to the hallway where the seniors' lockers were. We would sit down on the carpet with our backpacks and I'd watch for a cute boy to come by. The seniors had lunch later than we did and they were supposed to be in class, but we would hear people slamming their locker doors. That day was no different, not at first. Judith talked about her sister, Suzanne, and she helped me with my geometry homework. Like she always did, I guess. She ate some kind of sandwich on white bread and I had apple slices dipped in lots of peanut butter, the good crunchy kind. Right after we ate, I got the text from Banks Murphy.

"Alexis, let's get going here," my mother said and she pointed to my empty plate. She stabbed at the asparagus with silver tongs. They slipped and there was the violent sound of metal snapping against metal. I thought of Judith under the bleachers where I'd left her. There were metal posts holding up the bleachers and you'd hit them if you were backing up and not watching where you were going. A pan of baked beans was on the table next to the asparagus dish. It smelled sweet, but dark red ketchup was baked around the edges like dried blood. And there was dark-meat chicken with grease that gets into your skin and you can't get it off even after you wash your hands. And I thought, "There is no way I'm ever eating again. That is so disgusting. All of it."

Two Poems

Emily Ruth Isaacson

Virginia Dare's Mother

As I drive across the Croatoan Sound
Returning to the mainland
Over the Virginia Dare Memorial Bridge
I must ask you, Virginia,
What is it that you accomplished?
Why are you the one we remember?
Why do we focus on the mystery
Of your white doe
And not on the fate of your mother?

What was she like Virginia?
Did you live long enough—did she—
To get to know her?
Before the people ventured into
The great unknown waters
Again, across the Pamlico, the Albemarle
(Though you wouldn't have known it then)
Did she look towards Hatteras-Croatoan?
Or land in the boggy hills of Bertie County?
Did she even make it off the island
Along the barriers of our state?

And why was she there in the first place?
What drove the men in her life
To bring her here, laden with you, to the tiny
Isolated fort, meeting Manteo and Wanchese,
Shopping at t-shirt huts or
Eating frozen custard,
Peering across the sound to Bodie Island.

What kind of woman agrees
To leave everything she knows
To sail the vast blue deep
Towards a continent unknown,
Across unpotable water
To settle in a space barely
More habitable until the dredges
Come through, the concrete trucks
Pour miles of Highway
So she can walk between the markers
At Kitty Hawk, so she can chase the tourists
Across the dunes?

Virginia, there is a sign
On Highway 64 that tells us
The state of North Carolina
Disapproves of feeding the bears
Along the highway.

No word on what to do
Should we encounter a small,
Pure white doe.

Early Spring on Vaughan's Mill Road

The lone carrion bird
lays claim to his roadkill prey,
perched atop last night's doe
eschewing the smaller corpses,
mangled mammals—opposum? raccoon?
all martyrs to the pickup trucks
speeding through the nighttime
on the road snaking towards
the skeletal remains of downtown storefronts.
The sun rises over the distant treeline.
At the edge of the fallow fields
the new blades of grass
spring up through
the picked over, bleached ribs of winter.

A New Bike for Little Mike

Hardy Jones

A re you gonna fix Little Mike's bike?"

Little Mike's father heard his mama speaking to him, but he remained sitting on the weathered front porch drinking coffee, smoking a cigarette, and staring blankly into the summer sky.

"You've had time to fix it," his mama continued from inside the house.

Mike hadn't worked at the sawmill since some lumber fell on his right hand, crushing it, a month ago.

Mike's accident placed his job and his passion in jeopardy. The sawmill was his job, but Mike was an accordion player in a Cajun quintet—The Church Point Playboys—and since his accident he hadn't been able to play.

"Are you listening to me?" His mama was on the porch; the old wooden planks creaked under her feet.

"I heard you."

"Well are you?"

"*Oui.* Where is he?"

"He's out back cleaning the dog house."

Mike stamped out his cigarette on the porch and headed around the house to get his son so he could help fix the bike. Mike was supposed to have fixed his son's bike three months ago, but he put it off because he was setting aside a little of the money he made every week playing at different bars with his band, and he was going to use the money to get Little Mike a new bike for his birthday next month. But since his accident…

When Linda filed for the divorce a year ago, Mike took his son and lived in the Bon Temps Motor Lodge. He knew from his own parents' divorce, that judges gave custody to the mothers, so Mike figured their time at the Bon Temps would be his last chance to have his son live with him. Mike was going to stay at the motel till he could find a place, but after the accident, his money ran out and he went to his mama's. She lived off of her retirement from the school cafeteria and her Social

Security. Mike needed to get his hand looked at again, but he didn't have medical insurance and wouldn't feel right asking his Mom to pay for that too.

In the divorce, Linda got their apartment in town and Mike received custody of Little Mike because Linda, to all of Church Point's surprise, asked the court not to give her custody. Linda had been by to see Little Mike twice since the divorce. She picked him up on Friday both times and spent the entire weekend with him. Those visits were before Mike's accident.

When Mike was twelve, five years older than Little Mike is now, his father filed for divorce, and Mike's father had visitation rights every weekend, although his father usually only showed up one or two weekends a month. That was for the first year after the divorce. Then his father came around about one weekend every few months. A little later his father moved out of Church Point, and Mike hadn't seen his father since.

Little Mike was inside the dog house throwing hay out. "Get out of there, *cher ti garçon*. You're gonna be full of fleas. Use the rake to pull the hay out." Mike reached for the rake with his right hand, tried to grip it, but couldn't. He used his left hand and picked up the rake lying next to the dog house. "Do it like this. You see?" he said, pulling out a pile of hay.

"Yeah, Papa."

"Here, you do it. That's the way." Mike awkwardly lit a cigarette with his left hand and let out a cloud of smoke with a slow exhale. "When you finish this we'll start on your bike."

"All right!" Little Mike raked the hay out quicker.

Mike walked over to the shed where there was some hay stacked in bails for the milk cow, and broke off some with his good hand and carried it back to the dog house. "Take this and spread it around inside, *garçon*." Mike stuffed the hay that had been in the dog house into a garbage bag. "Take this garbage bag and set it by the road." Little Mike threw the bag over his shoulder and marched proudly to the road.

Mike carried the bike out of the shed with his good hand and set it on the left side of the front porch.

"Do you think we can fix it, Papa?"

"It'll take some work, but we can do it." Mike wasn't sure if this bike wasn't better off in a scrap heap. It was an older model bike: bent handle bars, a banana-seat, and faded red paint. "Go get me a crescent wrench

and my ratchet set from the shed. They're in the big metal tool box."
Little Mike ran to the shed and held his arms out like airplane wings.

Mike got down on his knees to get a better look at the problem. The
rear axle was loose, and to be fixed properly, it needed to be re-welded.
But that wasn't the real problem. The bike was just too small for his son.
This was the same bike Little Mike had since he was four, when Mike
bought it at a pawn shop and gave it to him for Christmas. In the last
three years Little Mike hit a growth spurt. He was going to be husky like
his papa.

Little Mike set the tool box down beside his papa, and Mike took the
wrench in his left hand, shook it, trying to get a feel for the tool, which
slipped off of the nut a few times before he got it turning smoothly.

"Mike, telephone," his mama yelled from the house.

"You see how I'm taking that nut off with the wrench?"

"Yeah, Papa."

"I want you to finish taking it off for me while I'm on the phone. Okay?"

"Yeah, Papa."

Mike stood back and watched his son struggle to get the wrench on
the nut. He wanted to yell at his son: It's so damn easy to put the wrench
on the nut and unscrew it. But he remembered how his father, before
the divorce, yelled when he would work with him, and Mike got to
where he hated working with his father. He remembered how scared he
would be trying to do something his father had just showed him, and
his father would stand over his shoulder, shouting sporadic curses in
English; and if he didn't hurry and do it correctly, his father would begin
a cursing tirade in French. Mike remembered his heart pounding and
his hands sweating as his father stood over him yelling, and that was
why he would not yell at Little Mike.

"Use both hands to guide the wrench, *cher ti garçon.*"

Little Mike steadied the wrench on the nut and pulled with all his
strength, but the wrench slipped off the nut. "Choke up on the handle.
It'll give you more control."

Little Mike looked up at his papa with the same worried look Mike
used to get on his face when he worked with his father. "Okay...okay,
Papa."

"Don't worry, *ti garçon.* Just take it slow. You're doing fine." Little Mike
choked up on the wrench and slowly it slid around and the nut turned.
"Now you've got it. When you finish with that nut, take the one on the

other side off."

Mike smiled at his son, stepped on to the front porch, and threw his cigarette in the yard before entering the house.

"It's Linda."

Mike cleared his throat. "Hello."

"I'm coming by later. Don't tell Little Mike, but I'm bringing him a birthday present."

"His birthday isn't until next month."

"I'll explain when I get there. Bye."

Mike placed a cigarette between his lips.

"Don't light that thing in here. You know I don't allow smoking in my house," his mama said, pointing her finger.

"Would you take Little Mike to the park, please?"

"What Linda done did now?"

"She's coming over. I don't want Little Mike here when she arrives."

"Why not? She is his mama. Maybe not much of one, but his still the same."

"I think she's leaving."

"Why you say that?"

"She's bringing Little Mike a birthday present."

"Oh. I see. I need to go by the grocery store anyway." She walked to the screen door. "Little Mike, come and go to the store with me. We'll stop by the park on the way home."

Little Mike stopped turning the wrench. "But I'm helping Papa right now, Maw-maw."

"It's all right, *cher ti garçon*. I'm going to take a break right now. We'll finish fixing your bike when you come back. Okay?"

"Okay, Papa."

"Now come wash your hands so you and Maw-maw can leave."

As they backed out of the driveway, Mike retook his seat on the front porch, lit another cigarette, and wondered how this encounter with Linda would go. The two previous times she came by to pick up Little Mike were okay. They were civil to each other. She quickly picked up Little Mike, quickly dropped him off, and didn't enter the house.

Now Linda pulled up in front of the house in her father's old Chevy truck, and Mike saw a new chrome racing bike tied in the bed of the truck. The late morning sun made the bike shine like a mirror.

Linda pushed the bike into the yard and leaned it against the front porch in front of the old bike.

"How you been?" she asked.

Mike eased his hurt hand into his pocket. "All right. You?"

"Fine. Just fine." Linda looked at the old bike. "I see you're finally working on Little Mike's bike."

"Can't afford to buy him a new one like other people."

Linda crossed her arms. "Don't start."

"I won't. I just want to know what's going on."

"I don't have to answer your questions anymore."

"Maybe not. But what about your son's? What do I tell him?"

"You don't have to tell Little Mike anything for me. I can talk to him myself."

"How you gonna do that when you're gone?"

Linda cut her dark brown eyes at Mike. "Who said I was going anywhere?"

"A birthday present this early is a signal that you ain't gonna be here when his birthday comes around next month."

Linda jumped on to the porch and got in Mike's face. "Stop it! I didn't want a child, you did. I wanted to get married, but I didn't want a family. He's your son; he has your name."

"You didn't want to get married. You just wanted out of your parents' house. You used me!"

"Like you didn't use me. Do you know what you put me through getting me pregnant?"

"I didn't do it by myself."

"You're right. You didn't. I'll give you that. But we hadn't even discussed having a child. We were still in high school for Christ's sake. You knew my parents wouldn't let me take the pill. You were supposed to be using condoms. I guess it broke, huh?"

"I didn't use them all of the time."

"You deliberately got me pregnant?"

"And you deliberately went along with it."

"I got a divorce so I wouldn't have to fight with you anymore. Where is Little Mike?"

"Just gonna give him a present and run? Is that it?" Mike shook his head.

Linda turned her back to Mike. "Nobody said I was running!"

"Then why are you here? Why a birthday present a month early?"

Linda dropped her head. "All right. Dammit! I'm leaving town, but I'm going to keep in contact."

"With me or Little Mike?"

Linda raised her head, turned around, and stared Mike in the eyes. "If I'm going to keep in touch with him, don't you think I'm going to have to keep in touch with you too? Don't act so stupid."

Linda walked closer to Mike. "The more I think about it, I believe you got me pregnant just to keep me around. You knew I was going to join the Navy after graduation. I had all the paper work prepared." Linda wagged her finger in his face. "That's what you did. You weren't going anywhere. No college or military for you. You were going to make it big with your band. I take back what I said about you wanting a family. You just wanted to anchor me to you."

"That's a lie. I love Little Mike. But you didn't want a child or a husband, just a way out of your parents' house."

"Well, I'm going into the Navy now. The lease is up on the apartment and I sold the furniture. I'm leaving today at noon and reporting to basic training in San Diego. I'm out of this hell-hole. You can stay here and play your damn squeeze-box."

"Can't." Mike held up his gnarled hand.

Linda cleared her throat softly. "You can use the hand, can't you?"

"I can close it partly and move my fingers, but only a little. That's no good for the accordion." Mike detected concern in Linda's voice. He thought there was concern in her eyes too, but he wasn't sure.

Linda took her eyes off of Mike's disfigured hand, took a deep breath, and said, "Now where's Little Mike?"

"He's not here."

"You knew I was coming. Why didn't you tell me on the phone he wasn't here?"

"He was when you called."

"Then why'd you let him leave?"

"I thought they'd be back by now. Mama took him to the store with her. I don't like her going out by herself."

"Then why didn't you go with her?"

"And leave Little Mike by himself?"

"You knew I was coming right over."

"You said you were coming over later. I assumed that meant this afternoon or this evening."

"Great. I've got a bus to catch and I still have to get some stuff from my parents' house and have them drop me off at the bus station."

"Well, it's only a little after ten. They'll be back in a little bit."

"How long ago did they leave?"

"Twenty minutes, I guess. You want to come in and have a cup of coffee?"

"I don't want any coffee! I want to give Little Mike his new bike. Damn you, Michael Trahan. You did this on purpose."

"What?"

"You knew I was coming and you didn't want me to see Little Mike."

"Have I stopped you from seeing him before?" Mike threw up his hands. "What does it matter? You didn't want Little Mike. You already said that."

"Wait!" Linda raised her finger at him. "I might not have wanted to get pregnant when I did, but I carried him for nine months, went through fourteen hours of labor for him to come in to the world. So don't tell me I don't love my child."

"He's mine. He's got my name, remember?"

"But he's got half of my blood. So he's half mine."

"You gave up your half!"

Linda stepped back. "Why are you using Little Mike to hurt me?

"You can't hurt that much. You're leaving, ain't you?"

"Yes. To make a life. I don't want to end up like my mother, tied down with a house full of kids. She's only able to talk about what she wanted to do with her life. But I am going to make the life I want."

"A life for yourself. Sounds selfish when you're responsible for a child."

"And what you're doing right now ain't selfish?"

"I'm protecting him. It's gonna be just him and me, so he might as well get used to it."

"Don't you think it was difficult for me not asking for custody? Do you know what it's like being afraid to look other women in the eye because of what they're saying about me? I hear old women, friends' of my mother's, mumbling about me when they see me in the grocery store."

"I want to ask you one thing, Mike. Why does everybody think I'm a bad parent for not having asked for custody? Why is it different for the man? You helped make him. You're just as responsible for him as I am."

"And I'm honoring my responsibility."

Linda turned her back to Mike and slowly stepped off the porch. She wiped away her tears and said, "Tell Little Mike happy birthday for me. I hope he enjoys the bike I bought him."

As Linda drove away, Mike lit a cigarette. When she was out of sight, he stepped off the porch and examined the new bike. "This looks a lot like the bike I was gonna buy him," Mike said to himself. He carried the old bike with his good hand to the road and set it next to the garbage bag full of hay.

Mike retook his seat on the front porch, drew on his cigarette, and couldn't wait for his son to get home.

Instrument

Mark Pritchard

Roy Pullen, who managed the Standard from four a.m. to noon, knew just where the church was, although he had never been there. Because of the Anointing, the church had become suddenly popular, then a local attraction, then a national phenomenon.

The people who stopped at the Standard station to get directions to the church assumed he attended it, because of its nearness. He didn't dissuade them. He knew that if he told them he didn't believe in the Anointing, that he didn't really go to church, that they would try to convert him to the love of Jesus and a new life.

But he didn't want to become like the muscular Christians with their minivans, their four children and exhausted-looking wives. They had to be upright before the Lord and be the head of the family, whereas Roy could clearly see they would much rather still be hanging with their buddies, going to Hooters on Friday nights, and being a backslidden, occasional dope-smoking gas station manager with a paid-for Camaro and seven units of community college.

But one morning, a young woman climbed out of her car and slid her credit card through the slot in the pump. Appraising her healthy blondness, Roy wandered over. "Anything I can help you with?" Roy asked.

She flashed him a big smile. "You might check to see if I'm lubricated," she said.

"Beg pardon?"

"Roy," she said, looking at his shirt. "That's nice; it reminds me of 'royal.' Are you royal, Roy?"

She was teasing him, a hopeful sign. "I'm a royal asshole, somebody said." His technique was to swear with girls as soon as possible; if they didn't seem to mind, he took it as a sign they would permit him other indiscretions.

She looked off to the side and smiled thinly. "My name is Lelani," she said. "I'm singing tonight at the Minnen Tabernacle." The pump cut off and she removed the nozzle and replaced it in the pump, without dripping.

She opened her car door and swung her butt and her legs in. "I'm going to do a couple of songs in the service tonight," she said. "Be nice if you came to hear me."

He stood looking after her, watching her Christian fish placard disappear into traffic.

He had met girls before who invited him to church. It was not unusual in this part of the country; an invitation to church or a casual testimony to the Lord's goodness was part of the people's everyday talk. This girl seemed to push it. "See if I'm lubricated?" He couldn't believe some strait-laced Christian chick would talk like that if she didn't mean it.

Lying in his bed after his shift ended, the summer heat bubbling outside the drawn curtains, Roy imagined gently checking to see if, indeed, she was lubricated.

The parking lot at the Minnen Tabernacle already had more than a hundred cars when he arrived, and a line of people snaked under a tent that had been set up to cover them from the sun. As the day ended they filed into the sanctuary.

Young men on a stage were playing rock instruments. People raised their hands and arms to heaven in receptive attitudes, and a few at the front were already swaying their heads deeply from side to side; they looked like kindergartners playing elephant.

There was no sign of Lelani. Roy moved to the end of an aisle, the better to slip out during the service if she didn't show up. Then he felt a heavy hand clap him on the shoulder. Startled, Roy turned to find a large, beaming man in a polo shirt striped to emphasize his width. "E. B. Bunting," the man announced, sticking out his hand.

"Roy Pullen," Roy said, and because the music was blaring out loudly at that moment, had to repeat it. "Roy!" he shouted into E.B. Bunting's ear.

Bunting let go of Roy's hand and swiftly grabbed his upper arm, as if he were going to throw him out of the building. With his other hand, Bunting made a little roof over Roy's head. "Jesus!" he exclaimed. "Bless this, your little brother ROY, as he enters into your temple! May the Holy Spirit fill Roy as you have so many others, that he may get a double measure of the FIRE that is sweeping this place! May it burn him, Lord—may it burn the sin out of him, and the drugs, and the sex, and the

television, and all things that are not pleasing to you, and may you FILL Roy with a spirit that makes him new. Now lead Roy to repentance and brokenness before you, Lord, make him an instrument of your spirit, and we praise you!"

E. B. Bunting's grip had tightened progressively during this prayer, until he threatened to lift Roy right off the floor. Roy had to latch on to Bunting's shoulder with his free hand, and this gesture of solidarity encouraged the minister to pray even harder. He went on at length about repentance and sin, and delved into Roy's personal life in such detail that it seemed the minister had been following him to Hooters and the Cineplex every night. The man seemed to feel so genuinely bad about Roy's sinning that Roy started to feel a little bad too, if only because Bunting seemed so torn up about it.

"And the evil thoughts, Lord!" Bunting confessed, seemingly on the verge of tears, "banish those thoughts right now." And Bunting actually smacked Roy on the forehead, not once but several times, as he repeated, "Banish the thoughts of sex! Banish the temptations of the Evil One! Banish the thoughts of pussy and girls and evil behavior, for this is your child, Lord..."

Roy was stunned by Bunting's blows, and the stranglehold on his arm, and couldn't believe the minister had actually said "pussy." The music had grown louder and more vigorous during Bunting's prayer, and now neared its climax. Everyone in the hall was singing at the tops of their lungs. The minister abruptly finished his prayer and released Roy, who fell into a seat.

The band came to a final chord and held it, thrumming louder and louder, as the crowd burst into shouts of praise and exclamations in tongues, creating a din that rattled Roy's brain more than E.B. Bunting's smacks on the head. The shouts turned into a roar, until it was no longer the sounds of individuals combined into a cheer, but a single cosmic tone that threatened to buckle the walls of the building. This was the Anointing. This was the movement of the Holy Spirit.

Finally, a minister on stage gave a signal, and the noise lessened and seemed to evaporate. Another, quieter prayer began, accompanied softly by the band's keyboard player. The minister spoke in slow, measured tones that lulled the audience while at the same time calling them to repentance. People around Roy were weeping now, still standing with their arms and hands raised to the skies, but in a sort of crushed, exhausted way, like a grove of trees after a hailstorm.

Still stunned by the thumping he had received, Roy wasn't paying much attention when a young woman began performing a syrupy pop song about how the Lord was there whenever she needed him to fill her with good things. Smirking, Roy reflected on how, if you listened to it a certain way, it sounded like she was singing about how happy she was that the Lord was porking her good and regular.

Then as the band began a new song, the girl started talking over the music, not so much about repentance but about changing your life. She had been trapped in an office job where the manager sexually harassed her. But when she accepted the Lord, he not only delivered her from that situation, but helped her pursue her true dream, to be a singer. Roy suddenly realized that the woman was Lelani, the girl at the gas station who had flirted with him. She had on stage makeup and wore a soft blue dress that made her look positively motherly, but in a sexy way, and Roy stared at her with new interest.

You too, could change your life, she said. Jesus didn't want you all hunched over and useless in a job where you were treated badly, a job any moron could do. "Jesus changes lives! He wants you to be everything the Father created you to be," Lelani exulted. "Think about it: were you created to do what you're doing now? Were you really meant to just sell insurance, or cars, or manage a gas station? Is that what the Lord Adonai, Great Creator God made you to be? You don't have to just get along in life. You can be the victorious child of God that is your birthright!"

Roy stood absolutely still. She was speaking to him. She saw him in the gas station today and somehow knew that it wasn't good enough for him. She had invited him here tonight, and knew he was here, and was saying these words to him, while the band repeated a chorus for the umpteenth time.

"What is it that God made you to be? You know! Deep inside you, you know! And the Lord knows also! For it is written that 'I know what you pray before you pray it.' What is it that you truly know you were created to be?"

Roy could scarcely breathe. He did have a secret dream. When Roy was a child, he had wanted to be a doctor. But when he got to Remer County Junior College and tried to register as pre-pre-med, the counselor had taken one look at his grades and laughed in his face. "I'll tell you something you could do, if you're interested in the medical field.

Not nursing—you probably couldn't handle that either. But you could be an EMT, an ambulance attendant. That's the sort of thing someone like you does." Ever since then, even after he had dropped out of the junior college, Roy had thought about this goal. Whenever ambulances came into the station, Roy hurried out to serve them himself, and shyly asked the EMTs about their work and their training.

"You can have that life-changing experience here! Tonight!" Lelani proclaimed. "But you have to give yourself to the Lord first! You have to call him Lord!" And finally, releasing the tension that had built up with chorus after chorus, the band returned to the verse of the song and Lelani began singing about this life-changing experience.

Roy felt as if a voice had whispered inside him to a secret self. He knew this to be his soul. The soul lived under all the crap inside him; the crap couldn't touch the soul, only stifle it, until a moment like this when you could reach down and pull it out like a puppy that had fallen into a ditch.

He prepared himself for some embarrassment. No doubt there would be some kind of altar call, and it would be necessary for him to confess his backslidden condition and give himself to Jesus. But he had done this twice before, as a teenager, and he knew it wasn't important. What was important was that this time somehow the ritual would take, and his life would be changed, and he could be an EMT. Maybe it was because of the Anointing, which could overwhelm the crap inside you and let the soul emerge, like the newly-cleansed, water-blasted driveway at the gas station.

Lelani finished her song and left the stage. Instead of a sermon and altar call, the minister who had led the shouting came out on to the stage with something that looked like a long horn. He lifted it to his lips and blew, and out came a flatulent squeal. The crowd reacted as if it were the most glorious fanfare they had ever heard; they broke into shouts of praise, and the speaking in tongues began again in spots around the room.

"The shofar has sounded!" exclaimed a man who had not been on stage before. He stood at the microphone with one hand lifted into the air as if it was being pulled up with a rope. "Let us now lift our voices against the powers of darkness! Let us battle in spiritual warfare against the armies of Satan!" There followed a jumble of prayers, shouts, tongues, wails and other noise. The volume and intensity didn't build into a single wave the way the shouting had; instead it formed a choppy sea of sound that made Roy a little woozy. A few people away from him, a middle-aged man dressed in a brown polyester jacket was rolling his head back and forth and side to side, uttering a growl that was relieved from time to time by a few nonsense consonants. Nearby, two teenage girls were bouncing up and down rhythmically like they were headbanging at a concert. Even the older woman next to Roy was making little chuffing sounds: "Achh...uchh...ooosh...gkwummmmch..."

Suddenly Lelani appeared by his side. She grabbed his hand and easily led him through the crowd to an alcove near the side of the stage.

"Lelani," he said. "I—I came like you said."

"You did, Roy. I'm glad you came. I want you to pray with me, Roy." She looked deeply into his eyes, her face close to his. She had washed off her stage makeup and stood before him glowing and looking fresh. "Repeat after me: Jesus, I want you."

"Jesus, I want you."

"Jesus, I want you to fill me up and make me your own."

"And make me your own, and an EMT."

Lelani said, "Roy, I just feel the spirit coming on. Put your hand on my stomach, right here. You know that's the place the spirit likes to reside. And I'm going to put my hand on your heart. And I know we're going to receive the Holy Spirit."

They swayed together, praying, their hands on each other. The rest of the room seemed to be dissolving into chaos, while they stood apart, wrapped in intimacy. Lelani's breathing deepened and she began undulating gently, pushing his hand a little lower on her stomach. Roy wasn't saying much more than "Oh God... Oh Jesus... Come into us." Lelani's prayer had also grown simpler, more rhythmic, and sometimes they said in unison, "Jesus." This thrilled them and made Lelani bear down on his hand a little more. He felt as if he was on the verge of something.

"Come, O Jesus," she gasped. "Come, O Jesus! O Jesus, oh—" and her prayer soared into a flight of tongues as her body vibrated and she jammed Roy's hand hard against her belly and began to pound against his chest with her fist.

"Oh Jesus," Roy said faintly, sweating hard, holding her. Did everybody in this church pray by hitting people?

After a time, she ceased vibrating and undulating and gasping. She released his aching hand and clasped it in hers. Looking into his eyes, she grinned at him. He smiled back, shy, confused. "May the Lord bless you, Roy," she said, and turned and disappeared into the crowd.

He only had time to open his mouth in amazement and she had vanished. He stood there for a few moments, bobbing in the ocean of noise and hands and spastic jerking back and forth. Then he left, stepping over a couple of people who were lying on the floor laughing uncontrollably.

Roy went to work at the Standard station as usual the next morning. He spent the hours of his shift quietly going about his duties, refraining from the usual horseplay, and pondering his experience. He knew he had not received the spirit the night before; but it had been promised and he now felt entitled to it. By the time he got off at noon, he had decided to go back to the Tabernacle to understand just what had happened.

After waiting a long time, he was shown into a small office marked Prayer Counseling. A minister in his 30s, named Windle, sat down with him and listened to Roy's recounting of the night before. He looked off to the side mostly, nodded to Roy when it was appropriate, and looked at his watch more than once. When Roy was finished telling about Lelani, and how she had been touched with the spirit and he hadn't been, Windle asked, "And what can I do for you, now that you've told me this?"

Roy was brought up short. "Well..." he stammered. "I want to receive the spirit, you know, because I want to change my life, and I believe Jesus changes lives."

Windle nodded. "You know, I think what happened there..."

"Roy."

"I think what happened, Roy, is that you were an instrument."

"Beg pardon?"

"An instrument. You said you laid your hands on this woman, and she received the Holy Spirit."

Roy nodded dumbly.

"Well, don't you see, Roy? She received the Holy Spirit through you."

Roy listened as the minister went on. "I think you have a gift of power. The ability to bring the spirit to others by the laying on of hands. A gift that many of us would envy. You can be used of God, Roy. Come with me."

Roy followed the minister to a small classroom. Inside Roy saw five or six women of varying ages, seated in folding chairs. "Why don't you see what you can do with this group?" Windle said, and without waiting for an answer, turned and left.

Roy stepped into the room and smiled. "Hello, ladies." Two of them were his age or younger, he noticed, and they all smiled back at him with varying degrees of shyness and hunger.

Her Prince Charming

Zachary Honey

The only thing of any particular interest in the small town was the bar. It had few regulars, but many temporary patrons of questionable moral quality. The drinks were cheap, but in enough quantity would bring about all the sensations of drunkenness. From one corner rang the sounds of the piano. From the opposite, men gambled away meager fortunes and from their lips wafted thick puffs of cigarette smoke. The turbid haze gave shape to the sharp rays of sunlight creeping in through the cracked shades. The old saloon was home to drunks and drifters, ranch-hands and law-dogs, and the occasional scuffle amongst the lot of them. Altercations were infrequent however, as the callous old cuss who owned the place wouldn't stand for any amount of rabble-rousin'. Most folks knew this; a few had the scars to prove it.

She had been a barmaid since she was very young, and was accustomed to unfamiliar faces and busy nights. All sorts came to this place, and she liked to imagine them all as on some big journey. The gunslinger hunting a valuable bounty. The hopeful prospectors out seeking a great fortune in the mountain streams. The Yankee who set up shop to take advantage of the poor fools come out to strike it rich. Truth-be-told they were all just men who liked strong whisky and forgetting troubled times but, ever the dreamer, she hoped one day to join them. She wished one of those brave men would sweep her away and they would run off in the dark of the night. Deep down though, she knew dreams were only dreams, and she stayed.

Tonight was as usual as they come. The later the hour, the louder the conversations and the more aggressive the men got toward her. As she scanned the busy bar for who to serve as well as who was too far gone, she noticed a tall figure leaning against one of the square, wooden pillars. Shadowed by the brim of his hat, she could not see his face but she was sure he was unfamiliar. A white puff of smoke erupted from his lips and the man beckoned with a cock of his head the woman to come closer. Nervously, she accepted.

As she approached, the man stepped forward and wrapped his arm around her, and placed his hand on the small of her back. His eyes stared into hers. He was more handsome than anyone she had ever known. His hair was tinged with grey and his eyes dark, but soft.

The piano changed to a soft waltz, and they danced. She heard nothing but her own slow, deep breaths. As they danced, their eyes remained unwaveringly locked and she wondered if he could be the one. The one who would take her away from everything. Away from the dirty bar. Away from all she hated. Her Prince Charming. The dance stopped at the bottom of the stairs and with one swift and fluid move the man bent and placed his arm behind the woman's knees and swept her upward off of her feet. He then carried her up the narrow, creaky stairs. In shock and in love the woman felt safe in the man's strong arms.

At last, they made it to a room. Her heart beat quickly in her chest. The man gently placed her on the bed. She could feel the constant ebb and flow of her own hot pulse as the man slowly unbuttoned his shirt. With one knee on the bed he hovered above the woman supported only by his perfectly defined arms. Gently, she ran her fingers down the man's rock-like chest and over the solid ripples of his stomach, until she gripped his belt-buckle and pulled him on top of her. As their bodies converged, so did their lips. A flash of heat and a wave of impetus ran down the woman's body, forcing upward her chest, then stomach and finally her hips. Her eyes were closed as he unbuttoned her blouse and then he ran his hand from the bottom of her calf slowly and smoothly up her thigh. Quickly the two were glistening with the sweat of ecstasy.

Suddenly and without warning, the man rolled off the bed and stumbled clumsily onto his feet. In a scramble he pulled up his dusty jeans and refastened the few remaining buttons of the tattered shirt, which only barely covered his bulging gut. With an unhooked belt, his pants held up with one hand, the remainder of his dirty clothes sloppily piled in his other arm, the man turned to the woman and tipped his sweat-stained hat toward her. She could barely see his crooked, yellow teeth through his wiry black beard as he gave her one last smile before he bumbled out of the room.

A thick lump formed in her throat as that oh-so-familiar depression washed over her face. But she didn't cry. She never cried anymore. The bills tossed carelessly on the mattress crumpled in her hands as she gathered them. Alone in that dark, dirty room she began to wonder who

Prince Charming would be tomorrow night.

Snout

of the

Alligator

Charles J. Beacham

It's funny to me that people don't know the difference between an alligator and a crocodile. Not funny in the sense of humor, but rather in the way of misunderstanding, when laughter is the accepted uncomfortable reply. Here, in the Lowcountry, there are a few ways to recognize an imposter of the local flavor of Southern heritage. One sure way is the name someone applies to the American alligator. Maybe it's because I grew up in the marshes and waterways where alligators are a constant threat, beings of which we were always aware. Usually, however, awareness came from a distance and by manner of careful admiration. Stories were often told of the disappearance of a man's champion beagle or a woman's prized Persian in the middle of the day. It was always concluded that an alligator devoured it. The event was devastating for the person who held the animal in such personal favor. But, such events are accepted as a sacrifice for living amidst the pungent saltwater marshes at the snout of the alligator.

Those born and raised here develop deep-seated reverence for this ancient reptile, the one that lived among dinosaurs, then survived them through stealth in the grand evolutionary story. For those born and raised here, the alligator symbolizes strength, the independence of a region cultivated from ancient roots. Those who show impatience or fear towards this creature, immediately reveal themselves to be outsiders - the uninitiated, transplants. But, who could blame them for their misunderstanding? The alligator, as a constant threat, is difficult to accept. It is also difficult for the unfamiliar, as I found out, to distinguish from an African crocodile.

The Man with the shotgun is a prime example. He is a former military man, like most in his generation. One of his service assignments relocated him to the Lowcountry many years ago. The slow, yet, flowing lifestyle of the area attracted him so much that when his service ended, he sought employment here. One of the many local paper mills, plentiful due to the surrounding pine forests, hired him for a high-ranking

position. Apparently, the military stint served him well, as he was extremely successful in the management of large-scale production. He rose through the social hierarchy, dined with corporate executives and city officials, and hunted fowl at the most-prized and well-stocked clubs along the riverbanks. And everyone knew about his success, whether they wanted to or not, because it was a steady source of his conversation.

One hunting club that The Man frequented was owned by my grandfather, Dee-Daw. The large acreage was dominated by pine forests bordering the marsh and river. From an early age, Dee-Daw took me there, regardless of season. In those times, he introduced me to earthly cycles, proper gun maintenance, to the possibility of self-sufficiency in partnership with nature. I came to know the reverence with which one must hunt to ensure that the energy given by the meat remained pure, not tainted with fear. During the fall, Dee-Daw spent his weekends at the club, tracking and hunting with friends or entertaining guests. Whenever I was allowed, I'd tag along. I enjoyed spending time among the pine trees, walking the forest carpet their needles created. I also enjoyed the miasmic marshes—the sulphur tickling my nose, the cattails swaying in the breeze, the mud oozing between my fingers and toes. My favorite part was being one of the men, hearing the tall tales they spun around the rock fire-pit as they cleaned their weapons. I noted how they took their guns apart, wiped each piece clean, oiled every surface, and reassembled them. When each man told a story, the glow of the fire spotlighted his face, his body. They relived previous kills, laughed as they smoked cigarettes and drank bourbon under the moonlight.

The Man with the shotgun was a frequent guest, because, quite simply, he was always ready for a kill. It was not uncommon to hear his voice around the fire-pit cursing "that damn crocodile," the one that often appeared on the small island's bank near the second of three large duck ponds. He lamented how he would never bring his prized pointers to that area "because they'd surely be devoured" by what he considered a useless beast. Such is the mindset of one who cannot connect the small point of the present to all the other points leading backward to the ancient, as was this case, The Man with the shotgun who was not raised in the Lowcountry.

One overcast autumn day, The Man couldn't take it any longer. His fear, though he would never term it as such, finally overcame rationality. He claimed an attempted attack on his grandson, a spacey and disinterested boy of thirteen, as they returned by foot from an early morning deer hunt. The other five men doubted the so-called attack, because this particular 'gator had never displayed such aggression in the past. Sure, a couple of young beagles disappeared in that area two seasons ago. It was naturally assumed by all that they had become 'gator-food. But this was considered sacrifice, sad yet necessary. In multiple sightings and close encounters with this particular alligator over the years, it never moved aggressively on any human being. Not to deny it from the realm of possibility. The primal desire for food is a powerful one. Regardless, The Man aimed to eliminate that "damn crocodile" as he always called it.

So, on that fateful day in late fall of my seventh year, The Man came tearing through the weekend's makeshift camp near the fire-pit to gather the implements necessary to subdue "that damn crocodile" forever. I sat on a log near the fire-pit eating oatmeal and watched the scene unfold. Followed slowly by his grandson, who was forced to hunt with Grandpa while visiting from some northern town. The Man entered the woodshed that served as storage for a variety of weapons and supplies. He picked through the available weapons until his eyes fell upon the shotgun. He stopped. In that moment, I knew his desire was not one of elimination for safety's sake, but rather of destruction. I thought it more a means to fill the void left by his own mistakes and weaknesses. He picked up the shotgun, cradled it against his chest, and tested the pump action. He would stop at nothing to establish complete dominion over the crocodile.

Along with the shotgun, The Man collected the proper shells, a large spool of strong thin rope, and a hunk of freshly-killed chicken to lure the beast. Dee-Daw, a man of considerable wilderness knowledge and hunting experience, tried to calm the outburst. I assumed him to be Dee-Daw's friend, since they always hung around each other at camp. Looking back, Dee-Daw simply tried to ensure the other hunters' safety from this man's misunderstanding the power of a gun.

Dee-Daw's dissuasion was unsuccessful. The Man ignored everyone as he hurriedly made preparation for his shining moment. Dee-Daw shadowed him closely to make sure he hurt no one other than the 'gator or himself.

"I'm gonna peg that fucking crocodile," he mumbled to himself as he fiddled with the shotgun's trigger, "...just like those yellow island nips."

"Aha!" he exclaimed as he maneuvered the trigger into the desired position, allowing for a quicker release—the 'gator would have less time to submerge. The Man handled the shotgun adeptly, experience from what I later discovered was an extended tour on some Pacific island during World War II. The hair-triggered pump-action shotgun was his preferred tool for destruction; it was the weapon he was trained to use so well in humidity and the squalor of war.

By this time, The Man's grandson had grown tired with the whole scene, and watched with little interest as the tirade progressed. He wandered to the fire-pit and sat down on a log near me. He nodded his head towards me and then stared at the crackling fire. Obviously, he had witnessed such anger from his grandfather before, as evidenced by his search for anything else on which to focus his attention.

Finally satisfied with his weapon, The Man boasted, "*Semper Fi!*" and marched off toward the island. Dee-Daw and two other men followed slowly behind him. I followed them. I cannot tell you why I followed that day, or why I was even allowed to at such an impressionable age. Maybe I should've taken heed from The Man's own grandson, when he refused to accompany his grandfather down that path. If I hadn't joined Dee-Daw and the two other men, I may never have understood the power of misplaced anger and the demolition it initiates.

We walked, the scowling outsider leading the rest of us in our silence. Squeaky rubber gaiters, aggressive mumbling, and leaf crackling footsteps were the only sounds intertwined with thoughts of the needless destruction waiting just ahead. After moving briskly for twenty minutes or so, The Man slowed as we neared the alligator's domain. It was apparent he had a plan, one that was likely efficient. He took the length of rope and tied the raw chicken tightly with a knot I hadn't before seen. The military training had served him well, for certain things, I suppose. While the rest of us stood near a perfect line of young pine saplings, he circled around to a boggy area of the pond, where the water's depth would not pose problems. From there, he trudged on in his tall rubber gaiters and swung the rope over his head like a lasso, eventually flinging the chicken successfully onto the mudbank at the edge of the small island. The trap was set. He waded back out of the bog and squatted in position near a mossy oak about ten yards from the trap. Then, we all waited.

It was the first of three times I would experience such a strange silence, when all life silences its song, in anticipation of the end of one of its own.

The moments passed slowly, each one more nerve-racking, expanding in duration. The stench of such a basic life-producing marshland filled my nose with the beauty of primal birth, but soon the sweet pungent smell would be replaced by one of destruction and emptiness. I saw Dee-Daw and the other two men exchange inquisitive looks, hoping that the alligator would not succumb to this enraged simpleton.

I saw the sly motion in the water, the ancient eyes rising to peer across the ripples, and the tail slowly whipping through the murk. I looked around to see if anyone else noticed, and I could tell that everyone did— everyone, that is, except the man responsible for this grand piece of theatre. After a few seconds, the 'gator's body was shining on the water, and The Man finally recognized the scapegoat of his rage. Nervous excitement rose through his sternum. He bobbled but recovered the shotgun as he quickly stood up to prepare for the prize shot he had chased for so long.

Without recognizing the audience, the alligator quickly glided through the muddy water, pulled its large muscular body upon the mud bank, and approached the meat with voracity. The Man tugged briskly on the rope, taunting the beast. This riled up the 'gator, sending it into a frenzy down across the sloping side of the bank. In seconds "that damn crocodile" would reach the bloody mess of chicken flesh and devour it, just like those people we used to see at the buffet after church on Sundays. A few seconds provided the window for The Man and his delusion, after which, the shot would not be so clean, or unfairly dirty, depending upon perception. The moment was nearing.

The alligator moved toward the chicken carcass. Simultaneously, The Man moved closer toward the crocodile, squatted down to his right knee, pumped the shotgun almost silently, and steadied it against his shoulder. In carnivorous frenzy, the alligator pounced the meat, staying within a certain spot illuminated by sunlight on an otherwise shadowed area of the bank. It death-rolled the carcass twice, tore into it with razor teeth. The distraction worked—The Man saw the shot he wanted. A cool calm overtook him, no doubt the result of a similar island thousands of miles away.

The Man focused his aiming eye, just like a good patriot killing some "fucking nip." He was frozen like one of the Revolutionary statues in the local downtown squares. His eyes and complexion glazed over, as any trained killer does when he enters the emotionless state.

Sensitive trigger. BOOM! He released himself from the fear, or so he thought. The alligator was hit with a furious velocity of shells at a prime location just below the shoulders. While the scaly body tensed with muscle spasm and writhed in anguish, the hole through its back was the deciding mark. The body convulsed for a few moments as the tail slapped, whipped, and thrashed the mud across the bank. Then the alligator lay motionless.

With the smoking shotgun in his hand, The Man shrieked with excitement, sprang up and down as if he had won the grand prize on Wheel of Fortune. "*Semper Fi*! I drilled you, you fucking crocodile, you slimy mother-fucker...I blew a hole clean through your fucking back you piece of prehistoric shit! *Semper Fi*! *Semper Fi*!"

I witnessed a crowning moment—The Man's eyes beamed, his cheeks rose, his face flushed. The joy he had found. Perhaps this was my first encounter with darkness.

I stood there motionless. Dee-Daw and the two other men also remained still. Unlike me, however, they were neither surprised nor shocked. They understood where fury can lead, especially when combined with weapons and skill. They had seen it before I suppose, in some different situation with a different irrationality and a different implement, but with the same intention.

The Man tried to share meat with the other men, but they all declined. Those familiar with the old-timers understand the importance of the creatures roaming the land, of food chains, and of the respect required to keep them viable. The Man harvested any piece of the alligator's body that would make good social theatre, and was forever seen around town telling the story of his victory, displaying his belts, boots. "Local crocodile," he boasted.

The hunting club was eventually sold off in a large-scale real estate deal designed to alleviate public concerns about a certain paper-maker's contamination of the local river. As part of the sale, Dee-Daw acquired a variety of objects from the club, one being the shotgun used to kill the alligator. He probably never envisioned the outcome it would wreak on my family. Unintended consequences, it seems, are the hurdles with which we struggle as society and individuals.

And so that sensitive trigger, the one connected to the barrel of the crocodile-killing shotgun, found its home within the family. When Dee-Daw passed, it was moved into the possession of my particular branch of the tree, and though I had no direct responsibility over it, I always knew its location. It haunted me from the gun cabinet. Destruction, finality: that powerful pump-action became the ultimate symbol of humankind's search to control both nature and itself. I remember thinking about The Man and the shotgun throughout childhood, how the two collided in a moment to inflict unnecessary harm. The sensitive trigger—a personal symbol of aggression, loss of innocence. The dichotomy, the duality of the self, the two ends—birth and death. Yet, in between is where life happens. It happened to me.

Love Like Dysphoria

A.G. Carpenter

The lord of the underworld sits in the VIP lounge, sipping bourbon neat out of a heavy glass tumbler. His lips move like a semi-literate attempting to read a book, but he isn't reading anything. Not even the menu of over-priced and ridiculously named drinks the hostess keeps waving at him.

He knows that his clumsy summons has nothing to do with the girl's arrival, but as usual, after he has repeated her name a few hundred times, she comes through the door.

Persephone.

Persephone.

Persephone.

All legs and thick brown hair, with curves that are almost too perfect for reality but in such modest proportion it is impossible to tell if she is beautiful by default or design.

A blonde nudges him to one side as she squeezes in next to Mercury, who is playing reluctant wing-man to the god of the dead tonight. Reluctant, but he is the one who suggested the plan to win the object of Hades' affection.

Blackmail.

Hades made protests about the ethical nature of their plan. It wouldn't be real love if she were forced and so on and so on. Deep down he is just relieved to have someone else to blame.

They drug her. Easy enough with Mercury buying the drinks. When she gets woozy, Hades helps her outside. Into his car. Up the stairs at the skeezy motel.

She is even more beautiful under her clothes. Milk-glass skin and rosy cheeks and nipples. Even her perfect curves turn out to be real to the touch, not plastic or salt-water under her flesh.

Persephone.

Persephone.

High enough to touch the ceiling, she doesn't protest when he begins

the list of obscenities he has fantasized over for months.

Mercury takes photos. And Hades, he fucks Persephone sideways.

They leave before she wakes up, but Mercury texts her a copy of one of the pics and Hades' phone number.

She doesn't call, at first. So Hades sends her a few more photos. Her on top. On bottom. On hands and knees while he plows her ass. He promises there are others. More graphic. More kinky. More publishable.

She calls. She is furious. She is willing to negotiate. Her family name, steeped in tradition and brown as the tobacco leaves they grow, will not take the stress of scandal.

They haggle over the details of the relationship and in the end they both lose. She spends every other day with him and they pretend to be a happy couple. In exchange he keeps the photos to himself. The rest of the time she does what she wants and he pretends he's okay with it. In exchange she doesn't bring her other lovers home.

It's a terrible arrangement from the very beginning and it just gets worse.

Hades grows sick of seeing her come home drunk and smelling of other men; spicy like Hispanics or earthy like the men from Cherokee. He gets weary of her belittling commentary on every aspect of his life. But he doesn't tire of her or the taste of her hot skin on his tongue.

One day he comes home and finds another man leaving. A young and handsome man who grins at Hades the way a teenager grins at his girlfriend's father. A man who slides into a low-hung sports car and speeds down the gravel drive in a swirl of gold magnolia leaves.

Persephone is upstairs in their bed, half-naked and completely sloshed. She says things she's said before, but this time they hit like fists.

Something breaks inside him. Not his heart, that would hurt. This is something like a cage door, like the chains holding a murderer tight.

Hades grabs a piece of fruit out of the bowl beside the bed. A pomegranate with ruby skin and blood red seeds. He stuffs it into her mouth in a desperate attempt to silence the bile pouring off her tongue. She shudders and subsides.

He sits on the edge of the bed for a moment staring at his hands, trying to catch his breath. Trying to contain the anger that scorches the back of his neck. And then he realizes she isn't breathing at all.

When he pulls the fruit out of her mouth there is a chunk missing. Wedging his finger down her throat he can just feel the missing seeds with the tip, but he cannot dislodge it.

He calls 9-1-1. He attempts the Heimlich maneuver and rescue breathing, but by the time the EMTs arrive, Persephone is brain dead.

Hades insists they keep her on life support. In case she recovers, he says with tears in his eyes.

He hires nurses to bathe her and change her soiled sheets and keep the IVs from getting infected.

At night he sends the help away for an hour or two. Throwing open the windows to let in the sweet song of tree frogs and the harsher chatter of cicadas. Pulling back the curtains so the warm green air can chase the smell of disinfectant from the room. He climbs into the bed and holds her in his arms and strokes her hair.

Now she doesn't fight against his touch. She doesn't flaunt her beauty and the knowledge that he won it only by trickery. She doesn't sigh or sneer when he makes love to her.

Persephone.

Persephone.

Hades knows she won't stay beautiful forever. Her skin will start to fade, her curves will sag, her body will turn skeletal from disuse. Someday he will grow tired of her and pull the plug.

He kisses her forehead.

Someday, but not tonight.

Long Finger from the Sky

Michael Russell

Robert and I took a day off from the shrieking stench of our jobs at a chicken farm. Seventeen thousand chickens had been trapped together in two barns, and we had to share their outraged captivity for ten hours a day. We were in northern Arkansas, a madhouse swirling in the boiling blood overflowing the brain of an angry, childish God. Or at least that's how it seemed. Perhaps God clotted our blood. Neither of us had taken a free day in weeks. If we took much time off, we'd have been fired, in which case neither of us could afford a home to not work in. Some nights after the end of a shift, I never wanted to smell or hear anything again.

Usually, the only freedom we could claim was taking a long truck drive together at night. There was nowhere to go, but at least the road was off the farm. We could pretend the farm didn't exist. There was nothing in the world except us, Robert's truck and the long, pulsating nerve of the road. During long drives late at night, up and down the lumpy, tentative mountains of the Ozark foothills, we could go for miles without seeing anyone else. I rested my head on Robert's right shoulder as he drove. I could almost relax and feel fully human until car lights jumped over the horizon. The shock always made us both jerk to opposite sides of the seat. Hiding was a reflex. I didn't have to think it through. Nobody could know I loved a man. And out here, everyone dearly wanted to know everyone else's business. Many people we knew could only attain true happiness by being offended and heartbroken over the depths to which their trashy neighbors had sunk, bless their hearts. Their God was nosy, too, peeking into our front door to say, "Nice soul you've got there. Be a shame if anything were to happen to it."

For our day off, we knew some abandoned property about fifteen miles from the farm. The last three miles was twisting dirt road, and Robert's truck threw a long snake of dust and pebbles behind us. The bumps and potholes in the road vibrated through me, making me bounce around and hold onto the passenger door. It felt like the road was giving us both a good riding. We looked into each other's eyes and laughed. We both knew the country so well, we were safe looking away from the road for a few seconds.

The only building on the property was a barn that insisted on remaining standing out of sheer orneriness. It might have been more rust and cobwebs than wood. Rattlesnakes lived there. Once, when we tried to enter, we heard a wall of rattling noise, a warning that the snakes didn't want to bite us, but they would if they had to. We made damn sure they didn't have to.

A few hundred feet beyond were several trees with leaves and branches so close to the ground that they all seemed to be taking a nap. Under the shelter of the biggest and lowest tree, I said, "I double dog dare you to strip naked and leave your clothes by that tree."

Robert almost hid that my idea scared him. "You're on! And I triple dog dare you to join me." That was exactly what I wanted to hear. We watched each other's body break free, ran away from our clothes and into a nearby pond. If anyone happened by, skinny dipping would be easy to explain. We didn't expect that anyone would come out here, but you never know.

Robert jumped on me, and we wrestled in the water. He was always stronger than me, but I put up a good fight. But when his nipples rubbed against mine, I kind of wanted to lose, to let him take me over.

Rain hit. It wasn't a gradual move up to a downpour. You'd have thought a lake had been floating in the air and fell without warning. We both laughed from the shock. Even though nobody else could hear, I whispered in Robert's ear, "Let's do it in the rain. Nobody will be out here to catch us. You don't have to be scared."

"I ain't scared..." Robert looked away, shaken, then grinned fit to drive away the rain. "I'm a gonna pound you into the mud." As I gasped from a finger, then two, I thought about how we had met in church. We had believed in the poison dripping throughout that building, and we thought we were monsters until we could see who we really were in each other's eyes. He saved me from Jesus. I had thought Jesus was the man for me, but he was just an abusive spouse who made me think I was nothing and would never amount to anything. Our divorce was full of barbed wire, but worth it.

The wind gave the fresh water waves. The hair rose on our necks. Robert looked up. "Um, John, I don't think this is just a rain storm." My

eyes followed him. Clouds uncurled their fingers, to reach out, to grab the sky and throw the wind at us. We were getting colder in the wind and water. We tried to grab our clothes, but they had blown away.

We ran to a small cave near the trees and had to crawl in on our hands and knees through a narrow tunnel. I was scared out of my mind, the raised hairs on my neck knowing that a storm like this often meant a tornado was coming. But somehow the sight of Robert's body was a comfort to me, as if his strength could hold back a storm. The light disappeared, and we couldn't feel the wind anymore. But we heard it ricochet through the tunnel, as if the storm were clawing at the rocks to grab and eat us. I had to comfort myself with the sharp echo of Robert's breath.

Shivering from the wet cold, we held each other for heat and to keep the bitter, choking dark from prying us apart. The wind screamed like an avenging angel, and the cave multiplied its shrieks. The cave was barely large enough for us to sit up. I felt Robert against my belly. I knew it made no sense, but his hard warmth made me feel safe. Ever since ninth grade, after he broke the arm of a boy who had bullied me at school for years, I smiled ear to ear just from knowing that my best friend existed. I could hide from the world with his big fingers inside me. I didn't have to feel scared anymore. If he ever left me, I would kill him. If he died, if anything happened to my beautiful man, I would tear the sky apart. Lightning would slash upward, shatter the earth into a trillion knives. The moon would fall out of the sky and land with a thunderclap that would empty the ocean. The only peace I ever knew was his arms holding me so tight I could barely breathe.

I turned around. Robert covered me, pressed his chest to my back. We were cold and wet and fed on each other's heat. The tornado had probably already passed by. Real tornadoes don't take their time to show themselves off like in the movies. They strike quickly and are gone within seconds. But the rain felt like staying, and we knew the cave was the safest place we could be. The flying knives outside couldn't touch us. I felt alive. As we rolled around, we disturbed a blind newt, which crawled over my ass to escape, just barely missing getting squished by Robert. I burst out laughing, and the cave walls bounced my voice back and forth. Robert was used to me laughing when we were alone together, so I didn't have to explain.

It made no sense, but I was scared to let go. My beloved might blow away in the storm. All those nights before we both knew how we felt, I worried about where he was, whether he was safe. I had wanted to call him many times a day, but if I had, he'd have thought I was cracked. But he stayed with me. He was scared of God but more scared of being lonely.

We fell asleep, too tired to care about the cold hard wet or how much our backs would hurt when we had to stand up again. Several hours later, Robert shook my shoulder to wake me up. "Hey, it's light out. Too quiet." There was no sound but our echoing breath and water dripping and running, as if the tornado had destroyed the world but left behind this dark hole.

As we crawled back out, the cave seemed to talk to us. Drip, drip, drip. As light greeted us, I imagined faces on the few visible rocks. Barely glimpsed, the faces seemed more vivid, their hard features melting, like a nightmare I couldn't remember.

We walked hand in hand back to the truck. Our bare feet made squelching sounds in the mud. But the truck was no longer there, and we had no idea where to look for it. All that was left was blinding sun on a small torn piece of metal. We'd have to make it back home naked.

Hands to ourselves, we walked several miles. A back porch had been torn off one home. It made me think of the time my back porch got blown away when I was ten. It was a thrilling adventure for a boy who had no idea what a new back porch would cost. Another building was in a thousand pieces. We saw the terrifying sun cast long shadows across the broken bones of houses. Crows keening. Vultures flying low. Drowned rattlesnakes. Broken skink tails. Catfish impaled on trees, seeming to swim in the air. Tall trees. Long rusty metal. Indigo snakes slithered in front of us. For the moment, there were no other people around to try to crazy glue their lives back together. Maybe they were fine, or maybe they died at home or were thrown into the sky.

We had somehow saved ourselves from being naked sacrifices to an imaginary god. But we were still trapped in Arkansas and wanted to fall off the Earth together.

A Sleeping Place

Place

A.A. Garrison

Of all the secrets in these woods, Benjamin sought the first he'd ever learned.

He journeyed into the wilderness, a gentle man of middle-age, looking every bit as sick as he was. His steps spoke: each recounted that gone autumn of his youth, when cancer meant nothing, when tomorrow included him, when *God* evoked mercy and warmth. The gun hung heavy in his pocket. The cave was a mile in.

Such beauty here, in contrast to Benjamin and the task at hand. In the years of his absence, the rolling mountain woods had lost none of their fidelity. He had feared them sparking the maudlin which had followed the diagnosis, but there were only memories, and a conflicted joy like coming home. Oaks and eruditic old pines oversaw his afternoon hike, affording a uniform shade that would degrade come fall. It had been so before, when he and Dana had adventured here.

Dana had been his next-door neighbor and childhood sweetheart, a strawberry blonde with just enough freckles. They had together found the cave, in Benjamin's tenth autumn. It had been the peak of the season, the trees aflame and the temperatures sublime, everywhere a rain of fire-colored leaves. The two had frequented the woods, which had changed little in the forty years since, but never had they ventured so far as that day. With pioneer courage, they had departed their usual route, for the wilds, thus finding the cave. Secreted in the mountainside like the orifice of some great beast, it had opened to a deep, black throat, the quietest spot either had ever known.

"It's a sleeping place," Dana had said, to which Benjamin had asked, "Do you mean a place to sleep or a place that's sleeping?" Adorably confused, Dana had answered, "Both, I guess." The two had then seated themselves on a convenient shelf of rock, just inside, where the daylight reached. There, they would deliberate their first kiss.

Benjamin, now grown, and haggard before his years, walked between hedgerows of rooted banks, over lanes that were almost paths. But

just almost: no one traveled these woods, then or now. He showed the ungainliness of a man alone, each step taken with minefield caution. The gun answered his every movement, jumping gamely in one pants pocket. It was summer, but the intact shade dissuaded the heat—not that it ever got too hot in the mountains, a fact he'd learned only after migrating to the city. Still, he sweat profusely, as he had this wicked last month. An adagio of birds and breeze swirled from all around, lending to the woods' anonymity. He was tempted to lose himself.

After an hour of his fragile walking, Benjamin breaked over a dead, fallen tree, the gray wood so much like stone. He yawned, and hated it; less than a mile in, and he was already needing a nap. He could feel the tumor in his head, just behind his right eyebrow, pulsing in dull escapements like a bad tooth. It was maddening, and violating: the enemy was inside him, and immune to all remedy, an opponent that had already won. He kneaded the plaintive area with a frail hand, cutting back swells of sweat.

While resting, he again reviewed the preparations he'd taken. The tumor had struck him forgetful, dangerously so.

His wife, Dana's adult successor, was named Pamela, and she knew only of the headaches, not the diagnosis. Nor did she know of Benjamin's recent "retirement." He'd told her he was leaving the country on business, which wasn't so absurd. Before this whole mess, Benjamin had played lawyer for a respectable firm with more than a few overseas clients, and Pam had grown accustomed to such travel. She'd kissed him goodbye, as always, with an "I love you" and a "Be safe," and he'd returned the sentiment, by some miracle repressing tears. To complete the illusion, he'd purchased a plane ticket in his name and left the receipt conspicuously on his desk blotter, along with some of their old love letters. He'd thought of writing a new one—because he did love Pamela, was doing this *for* her—but it would've been too obvious. She and the kids would have questions, as a matter of course; but they could never know.

Never.

Benjamin once more ran through the rest of his scheme—the bus ticket, the cab fares, the hat-and-sunglasses disguise he'd worn on his way to the woods—and he seemed to have covered his bases, rendering his sojourn to the mountains as untraceable as possible. At least, as far as he could tell. In the last month, his world had become a soupy limbo, something between senility and nightmare. His thoughts had turned traitor, untrustworthy even to himself—*especially* to himself. He'd recently gotten lost in the subway. Continence had become a private war. Simple signs were now puzzling riddles. He'd started keeping a notepad in his pocket, and it was his best friend. He would be indignant, if only he could remember to be.

He stood from the deadfall, with some effort, and continued toward the cave. Remembering the cave was, thankfully, one thing he could count on, if the only; its location was certain to him, in a calm, uncomplicated way, how a dream must see its dreamer. He resumed his punctilious walk, the gun whacking his thigh like a pocketful of pennies. It felt to weigh a ton or more.

The terrain was unaccommodating to his compromised feet, but he managed, mincing his steps and grabbing onto the stouter vegetation. The scenery was alive to him in a way nothing had been since the tumor, whispering of that season when he was whole and unafraid. The woods were familiar, strikingly so, despite his indisposition and the passage of time. Though showing the expected growth, the mountain was otherwise a window to the past. There was the babbling stream he and little Dana had hopscotched across; the gentle slope now precarious to him; the sunny glade opening to a majestic surround of Appalachians. He happened across a doe carcass, and felt an odd camaraderie. The sight stirred tears, but he forgot the animal before it could register, like everything nowadays.

Benjamin made the cave by late afternoon.

There was a panicked moment when he approached his destination and saw nothing. He remembered the cave mouth as a craggy slit commanding some pines and a small ravine, interrupting the mountainside like a garage. He saw the ravine and the pines, plus other fixtures he'd forgotten until then; just no cave. Then he discerned a quiet blackness behind a drape of roots and moss, alluding to space. Yards from it, he was met with a breath of cool air, phenomenally soothing, and he knew there had been no mistake. The opening was far smaller now, the woods having healed over it, but he managed through. Benjamin had recently lost weight.

The cave mouth opened to the space hinted at from outside. The daylight was stymied by the canopy, then more so by the natural portiere of vegetation, striking the cave an almost inviolate black. It was equally silent, the forest's ambience gaining no purchase here. A sleeping place indeed.

Benjamin fumbled a flashlight from the pocket not holding the gun, and clicked it on, cutting a flesh-colored circle in the dark. The floor was smooth and curvaceous, so much poured cement, the walls similarly so. It was eerily clean; the cave had, apparently, remained a secret to all but he and his little paramour. He aimed the light straight ahead and it disappeared in the black, showing little more than a wrestling shaft of dust. The ceiling opened up the deeper the cave went, conspiring with the sloped floor to create a cathedral attitude. Benjamin felt to be at the tip of a massive funnel.

After two careful steps, he came to the couch of rock on which he and Dana had shared their first kiss. Groaning, he collapsed more than sat, and the memory came like lightning, betraying his infiltrated brain. The children had perched mutually on the rock, like it was the very reason for their foray, and a quiet awkwardness had followed, the two glancing nervously about the gloom. He'd been uncertain in the moment, unsure of whether he should or shouldn't, or what to do if he should. Then, like magic, his lips had been on hers, moist and electric and the sweet of watermelon. They'd stared at one another after, searching for clues—then kissed again and again, holding hands with a delicacy which cannot be repeated.

As with the cave, the passionate experiment had remained their secret. It would not be spoken of afterward, like some crime they hoped to erase with silence. Then, a month later, Dana had moved away, and he'd never seen her again. They had written letters, but only a few, and these perfunctory at best. He'd thought of her, naturally, but life had gone on, and adolescence had buried her completely. He would every so often dream of returning to the cave, but never under such morbid circumstances.

The tears came now. The tumor eased back some, as if antidoted by the emotion. The memories of him and Dana soon faded, replaced by those of his past wrongs—pick a wrong, any wrong. They were constantly on his mind as of late, as he imagined it was for anybody toward the end. Along with a revised will, he'd written letters over the last month, a host of them, to everyone he had conceivably offended in his fifty years, however petty. A few had required some tracking down—a herculean task in his sick present—but he'd done it, amassing a stack kept locked in his office. He'd parceled them out a few at a time, as not to raise suspicion, getting the last off just before catching his bus. However, even after all those sorries, there was no sense of atonement, no closure. His life's transgressions had never bothered him before the tumor, when he had his wiring intact—and, he supposed, his self-delusion. But now, they were crushing, indictments against him, each one alive and pointing.

It was hell, but it was ending.

Benjamin slid the gun from his pants pocket and held it solemnly in both hands. It was a small black revolver, purchased discreetly through a contact of his—one perk of being a criminal-defense lawyer, having "contacts" when one needed them. It was menacing, the gun, almost a living thing. He'd never touched one before, even when growing up in the mountains. Benjamin had been forced to get a quick tutorial from the crook he'd bought it from, detailing the safety and the chambers and the cock. The man had instructed him on cleaning it, also, but Benjamin had politely ignored that part. The gun was loaded with six rounds, five more than he would foreseeably need.

He killed the flashlight, discarded it to the floor, and held audience with the darkness, kept company by the gun and his tumor. It was surprisingly relaxing, something like sleep, and he kept thinking of Dana's words: *It's a sleeping place.* She'd guessed it was both a place for sleeping and a place that slept, and Benjamin guessed she was right.

Then, from nowhere, he was babbling—another gift of the cancer. Crying, stammering, he spoke aloud the names of his wife and children, who could never know—said he loved them and he was sorry, that there was no other way, could they ever forgive him? He spoke no different than if they were present and watching, the words echoing into the cave's false night. With this, the tumor surged big, as if to attack.

Soon, however, the words ran out. It was time.

On that cool shelf of rock where he'd kissed a girl in another life, Benjamin then lay down for the last time. He cocked the gun, and employed it with an unimportant noise, to sleep. Once the echoes had died off, the cave joined him in his slumber.

The
Phrenologist

Shane K. Bernard

"I have noticed for a long time that those who deny the intellectual importance of the volume of the brain have, in general, small heads."

— M. de Jouvencel, "Discussion on the Brain,"
Bulletin of the Paris Anthropological Society, *1861*

Doctor Pierre Maturin, a son of France, hailed from a family that for generations had produced noted physicians. He earned his degrees from the Sorbonne and the fashionable university at Edinburgh. He subsequently returned to Paris to practice as a surgeon, but, finding the competition discouraging, sailed to New Orleans in the summer of 1850, where he established himself as a general practitioner. He set up his office on the corner of Chartres and Conti, in a small stucco building adjacent to the Slave Exchange. This proved a fortunate site for the young physician, for prospective buyers often sought his services as a medical examiner of slaves. One soon found the following advertisement in the local newspapers:

> *SLAVEHOLDERS! PROTECT YOUR INVESTMENTS!*
> *Owners or buyers wishing to ensure the health of laborers*
> *will do well by contacting me at 444 Rue Chartres.* — *Dr.*
> *P. Maturin*

Maturin shortly became known as a specialist in the examination and treatment of slaves, and his newfound affluence gave him much leisure time to occupy as he pleased. This he employed in furthering his knowledge of medicine and physiology, and through his reading and correspondence he developed an interest in the budding field of craniometry, especially in regard to its function in determining mental capacity. "I have begun to accrue a collection of skulls," he informed a colleague in France, "and will soon commence research on the current question of brain size and its relation to intelligence . . . what has become the new science of 'phrenology.'"

Maturin's prime phrenological interests were of a racial nature, formulated through observations made during his months as a medical examiner of the black race. As he wrote to his colleague, "I have found it to be a peculiar characteristic of the craniofacial structure of the Negro, that the jaw is much larger than that of the average white man, and that the back of the cranium—that part we call the *occiput*—is much more extensive in the darker race. It is my supposition that such anatomical distinctions, especially that of the skull, have a direct correlation to the obviously inferior intelligence of the Negro."

He started his phrenological inquiry by devising and calibrating a special pair of calipers, which he wielded to measure, record, and tabulate the sizes of the twenty-two skulls in his collection. He realized that such a sparse number of crania would hardly provide enough data for his research, so he began to include such measurements as part of every medical examination. This system worked well, because heads of the living were easier to borrow than those of the dead, and nearly as accurate to evaluate.

Maturin soon possessed a voluminous index of the cranial measurements of all his recent patients. Unfortunately, he had neglected to gather similar measurements for whites, whom he intended to use as his criteria. Maturin now subjugated every white client and acquaintance to his silver calipers, that he might, as he told them, "record for posterity the size of their splendid crania" and simultaneously advance his vital scientific inquiry. After six months, he had indexed three hundred fifty white crania, nearly equal to the number of crania he had previously measured of the black race.

When all the recorded sizes had been averaged, Maturin discovered to his disbelief no apparent different between the sizes of black and white crania. He informed an acquaintance, "My method of measurement must be at fault, else the figures should have reflected what is plainly the truth. I have decided to abandon the caliper method and, instead, to employ a more direct means of determining the size of the brain once held—I write 'once held,' mind you, because my new method of direct measurement demands that I return to the use of skulls."

To the same acquaintance he described this "new method of direct

measurement": "I have found a more accurate and simpler method, which I call 'internal evaluation,' the only fault of which lies in the need for a multitude of skulls. This method consists of filling each individual cranium through the hole at the base of the occiput—this hole we call the *foramen magnum*—with a medium, which is then emptied into a calibrated vessel. This reveals the volume of the cranium and, therefore, the exact size of the brain it once contained."

He added, "I have experimented of late with a variety of media, these ranging from water to molasses to mustard seed. But I have found the most reliable medium to be lead shot, particularly of the size called 'BB,' which is one-eighth-inch in diameter. Using this medium during trial measurements, the results never varied greater than one-one hundredths of a cubic inch no matter how many times I repeated the experiment. I might add that lead shot does not leak through small fractures as water is apt to do, is not so thick as to remain inside the cranium as molasses, and does not flatten like mustard seed. It is in my opinion the ideal medium."

As to his shortage of skulls, Maturin solved this problem by commissioning the city's criminal element to plunder the graves of paupers and slaves. It did so nightly for several weeks, appearing at midnight in the cul-de-sac behind the physician's office with cottonade bags of skulls, which Maturin purchased, naturally, on a per capita basis. After two months he accrued a gruesome collection of four hundred thirty-six skulls, half of which came from white subjects, half from black.

He kept these skulls locked in the musty garret of his office, the flat so thickly piled with jawless specimens that it resembled some kind of bizarre shrine or a primitive ossuary. A closer examination, however, revealed his methodology: Each cranium bore a tag, numbered in the doctor's ornate calligraphy, and sat on shelves on either side of the room according to race—one side of the room for "Caucasoid," as a placard read, the other for "Negroid."

In the center of the room sat a rough-hewn cypress table, and on this table Maturin laid out an inkwell and pen, a hardbound volume of ruled but otherwise blank accounting paper, a calibrated copper basin, and a small dovetailed wooden box containing five pounds of gleaming lead shot.

The considerable number of skulls to be evaluated required the hiring of an assistant. Maturin selected Thomas Broughton, a young northern transplant to the city and a recent graduate of the medical school at Philadelphia. The research began shortly after Broughton's arrival, in late August 1854.

According to Maturin's records, the first skull he examined on that first night of research came from a white male. Pouring handful after handful of lead shot into the skull, Maturin topped off the specimen, a few extraneous pellets bouncing and clattering on the hardwood floor, and called out a number, which Broughton recorded as "82 in³"—that is, 82 cubic inches.

He next chose the skull of a black male, which, he noted more than once with a hint of irony, appeared (except for minor differences in the brow and temple) no different on the surface than that of a Caucasian. "All are white, once stripped of flesh, are they not?" he quipped. He measured the skull, registering 81 cubic inches. Maturin later recorded his thoughts at that moment, confessing, "I considered the similar volume of these two crania to be at first dismaying—but decided after a moment's pause that either the black skull was unusually large or that the white skull was unusually small. Therefore, I reluctantly listed these results, or, rather, called them out to Broughton to record, and advanced to the next two skulls with high expectations."

Maturin chose the skull of a white subject, carefully filled and then emptied it of shot, and called out, "83 cubic inches." He then measured a skull from "the darker shelves," as he called them, and that cranium registered, to his annoyance, 85 cubic inches. With affected coolness, he continued to measure away into the night and early morning—much longer than Broughton had been led to believe they would work that evening—and recorded the volumes of over a hundred skulls by the end of the first session. "The results were disturbing," admitted Maturin to a colleague. "Of the one hundred thirty-six crania I measured, none of the white specimens contained a notably greater volume than that of the Negro specimens, the average for both being exactly 82 cubic inches."

Maturin delayed the next session with Broughton while pondering the curious outcome of that initial night's inquiry. He consulted the newest works on anatomy, imported from Europe and the North, to no avail. Yet one night, as he lay between sleep and wake, the doctor realized a terrible error in his procedure. "It struck me!" he later recorded. "It struck me as though I had been enlightened by divine revelation! The questionable measurements stemmed from this oversight: Whites are endowed with a larger *frontalis*—that part of the skull that houses the intellect—while that of the Negro is burdened with a larger *occiput*—that part housing the animal instinct. Therefore, in order to yield the correct measurements, I would have to adjust the actual volume of the Negro crania by *discounting* that amount representing the massive occipital region. This I did, and the results were most revealing."

Maturin published his results in a book he titled *Crania Americana*. In the introduction the doctor asserted, "It was not my intention to prove the white man superior to the black. Indeed, I conducted my work from a most objective, unprejudiced vantage, making a conscious effort to avoid any *a priori* conclusions." He ended his preface with the assurance, "I will now allow the facts to show whatever they will."

In the first chapter, Maturin reproduced the following chart, revealing the essence of his research:

Table 1.1. — General Summary of Cranial Capacity by Race		
Race	Cranial Capacity (In^3)	No. Crania Measured
Caucasian	95	210
Negro	88	226

"It cannot now be denied," Maturin concluded in the final pages of his study, "that the white race is intellectually superior to the black, for as my figures reveal, the average white cranium boasts an entire seven cubic inches more brain matter than that of the darker race. This 'surplus' is to be found in the larger frontalis of the white cranium, which accounts for the white race's intellectual superiority."

The scientific and medical communities, not to mention the general public, received *Crania Americana* with enthusiasm, elevating Maturin to the status of celebrity scholar. He amassed a small fortune through sales of his book, as well as by hawking pamphlets, articles, and essays aimed at uninitiated but curious readers. He toured the southern lecture circuit, filling university auditoriums, town halls, and churches. His office became a local landmark, a site for all sojourners to see. And it was well known among the young ladies of the city that Maturin was a bachelor. As such, wealthy fathers petitioned him to attend their daughters' lavish debutant balls.

The doctor, however, having been inspired by his mad success, expressed less interest in courtship than in increasing his wealth and fame.

Amid his plans for an even greater phrenological survey—titled *Crania Mundi*, it would compare skulls from numerous racial and ethnic types gathered worldwide—his reputation suffered a dizzying blow. Several scientists, it seems, while attempting to copy Maturin's experiments, yielded results to the contrary. Reports of these discrepancies quickly circulated throughout the scientific community and made their way into the national press.

When word arrived in New Orleans, Maturin hastened to defend himself, submitting a written response to the *Picayune*, the *True Delta*, the *Abeille de la Nouvelle-Orléans*, and all the other local papers, both in English and French. "It is no doubt known to all," he penned, "that I have been accused of 'fudging' my research, of falsifying the results presented in my *Crania Americana*. I have nothing to say of these *canards* except that they are lies spawned of the malice and envy of my many rivals. I refuse to be stirred by such accusations and will continue my research with the knowledge and conviction that the results I yield are scientifically valid and true."

The day after Maturin's letter ran in the local press, an unexpected riposte appeared in the city's several papers. Its author, the young medical assistant Thomas Broughton, stated:

> *I wish to respond to Doctor Pierre Maturin's statement that appeared in an earlier edition of your paper. I have had the experience of laboring beside Doctor Maturin during the early stages of his phrenological inquiry, and I wish to express my knowledge of his research methods.*

> *Doctor Maturin began his investigation on the night of August 24 of this year; I was present as his aide. As the doctor has claimed, he used the lead shot method described in* Crania Americana. *Contrary to the results published in his book, however, the cranial measurements of whites and negroes exhibited no noteworthy differences in volume.*

> *As the experiment continued, and as the results persisted in reflecting no differences in skull size, Doctor Maturin became disconcerted. When it became clear that his prejudiced presuppositions were entirely incorrect, he*

lost all ascendancy over himself. Grabbing a pestle used in his pharmaceutics, he forcefully packed lead shot into a white cranium and followed this action by violently shaking the skull to settle its contents. He then loaded more shot into the skull, ramming the pellets like a soldier franticly loading the barrel of his rifle under fire, sometimes cracking the skulls open at the fissures and spilling led shot by the hundreds onto the laboratory floor. Finally, he emptied the quantity of lead into a vessel for measurement, calling out the numbers for me to record, and occasionally rounding those numbers up slightly. It was in this deceitful manner that Doctor Maturin obtained results to his liking, for he was able in this slipshod method to increase the volume of the average white crania by many cubic inches.

As for my own role in the matter, Maturin relieved me of my duties that same night after I protested his dishonesty. My only fault, I believe, is in failing to reveal my knowledge of the incident prior to the present.

Maturin did not know what to do. He snatched up a pistol and considered a duel, or simply shooting Broughton outright, for the man was no gentleman, clearly, and hardly deserved an honorable end. Perspiring, panicking, he threw down the weapon. He picked it up again, hesitated, then flew to his garret laboratory and, gasping the pistol by its barrel, brought down its burnished grip on his collection of skulls. No sooner had he destroyed all four hundred thirty-six when Maturin collapsed dead upon the hardwood floor. An autopsy revealed the cause of death to be apoplexy.

It had been Maturin's request that the size of his brain be evaluated on death. Its volume came to 85 cubic inches—three cubic inches smaller, according to the Doctor's own mismeasure of man, than that of the average Negro.

Contributors

Heather Bell Adams grew up in Hendersonville, North Carolina and now lives in Raleigh, North Carolina with her husband, Geoff, and their son, Davis. A graduate of Duke University and Duke University School of Law, she is a lawyer practicing business litigation with an Atlanta-based law firm. Heather has published personal essays, poetry, and short fiction in a variety of online and print publications. She is a member of the North Carolina Writers Network, the North Carolina Poetry Society, and the Appalachian Writers Association.

Charles Beacham's vehicles include short stories, essays, and an upcoming novel–tentatively entitled *Sensitive Triggers*–a tale of the South's dark underbelly and a man's descent into schizophrenia. Charles holds undergraduate and graduate degrees unrelated to literature, and applies this knowledge to his writing where applicable. Charles currently writes from the foothills of North Georgia, where he resides with his lady, son, two dogs, and multiple shadows.

A Cajun from south Louisiana, **Shane K. Bernard** is a historian whose nonfiction works include *The Cajuns: Americanization of a People*, *Swamp Pop: Cajun and Creole Rhythm and Blues*, *Cajuns and Their Acadian Ancestors: A Young Reader's History* (recently translated into French) and *Tabasco: An Illustrated History*. He lives in New Iberia, Louisiana, along Bayou Teche.

A.G. Carpenter lives in the southern United States where she spends her days herding cats and a lively four year old. By night she writes fiction of (and for) all sorts. Her micro fiction has been published at

One Forty Fiction, *Cuento Magazine* and *Trapeze Magazine*. Her longer works have been published or are forthcoming at *Daily Science Fiction*, *Goldfish Grimm's Spicy Fiction Sushi*, *Stupefying Stories Showcase*, *Abyss & Apex*, and *The Beast Within 4: Gears and Growls*. She is querying a steampunk novel about magic, machinery and murder.

Caitlin Cauley is a NC born and bred, NC State alum, current barista-without-a-cause who works on writing on the side. Living in Raleigh and occupying the space somewhere between bohemian and bourgeois all while striving for good old Southern manners, pronouncing "pen" and "pin" the same way, and adding at least two extra syllables to her four-letter words.

Brian Centrone is the author of the novel *An Ordinary Boy* and the short story collections *I Voted for Biddy Schumacher: Mismatched Tales from the Mind of Brian Centrone* and *Erotica*. Four of his One-Act plays have been produced for the stage as part of the National Endowment for the Arts' *The Big Read* program. His writing has appeared in numerous anthologies, literary and arts journals, newspapers, and online. He is the Co-Founder and Publisher of New Lit Salon Press and has taught writing and literature at The Massillon Museum, SUNY/Westchester Community College, and New York University. Visit Brian at www.briancentrone.com and follow him @briancentrone.

A.A. Garrison is a twenty-nine-year-old man living in the mountains of North Carolina, where he writes and does landscaping work. His short fiction, from speculative to literary to experimental, has appeared in dozens of zines, anthologies, and web journals, published in America, Canada, and abroad. Also, his fiction has appeared on the *Pseudopod* horror webcast. He is the author of the post-apocalyptic horror novel, *The End of Jack Cruz* from Montag Press, which is soon to be made into a play of the same name. He is currently preparing his other novels for publication.

Zach Honey is a North Carolina born, Montana native. After growing up in the small, no-stoplight town of Darby, Montana, he graduated from Montana State University with duel degrees in Film and Philosophy, and a minor in English Writing. Zach has written and directed two short films and one one-act play. Currently, he is a graduate student of Philosophy at the University of Nottingham in England, focusing on Aesthetics and the Philosophy of Film. Upon the completion of his course in September, 2013, he will return to the States and start his next big adventure, whatever that may be.

Primarily a literary scholar, professor and poet, **Emily Isaacson** also spends time playing with photography. Her poetry has appeared most recently on the website of the *Pacifica Literary Review*; her most recent scholarly work is in the CEA Forum. For work, she teaches literature and will begin a new appointment at Heidelberg University in Ohio in the fall of 2013.

Hardy Jones received an MFA from the University of Memphis and a Ph.D. in Creative Writing and American Literature from the University of Louisiana at Lafayette. He has published thirty pieces of short fiction and creative nonfiction in journals, and he has been awarded two grants. His memoir *People of the Good God* is forthcoming from Mongrel Empire Press. He is an Associate Professor of English and the Director of Creative Writing at Cameron University.

Nathan Mark Phillips is a digital artist who lives in the Tampa Bay area of Florida within the city of New Port Richey. His hometown is Cleveland, Tennessee. His background has significant impact on his thoughts as expressed in his Art: Nathan is from the South; He is a student of theology, psychology and sociology; and enjoys Pop Culture. He has spent his professional life working in human services with the severely mentally ill, those impacted by substance abuse or family crisis. He lives a very rich and happy life with his partner of 19 years, the best of friends and a wonderful family. (Photo by Elizabeth Gordon)

Mark Pritchard is the author of two collections of sex stories, *How I Adore You* and *Too Beautiful and Other Stories*. He lives in San Francisco and works on novels.

Eryk Pruitt is a screenwriter, author and filmmaker living in Durham, NC with his wife Lana and cat Busey. His short film *FOODIE* has won film festivals across the United States. His fiction has appeared in *The*

Avalon Literary Review, Speculative Edge, Mad Scientist Review, and *Pantheon Magazine*, among others. He currently is writing for the stage and shopping his first novel.

Michael Russell has lived in Arkansas, Philly, and Portland, Maine. Next year, he and his husband plan to move to New Hampshire. For five years, he taught English in a rough Philly inner city high school. So far, he has written one novel, *First Floor on Fire*, and has written and illustrated one children's book, *I Don't Fit*. In the works are another children's book, *Leopard and Mouse: Cats Fight Dinosaurs*, and a sci-fi southern memoir, *Indigo Snakes Are Flying*.

Jordan M. Scoggins, also known as luke kurtis, is a Georgia-born interdisciplinary artist. His work has appeared in several publications including *The Emerson Review, Encounters, Georgia Backroads, Iceland Review, The Red Truck Review, Skin to Skin, S/tick*, and *The Walker County Messenger*. Other publications include his books *The Language of History* and *let us prey* (featured in RikArt Artist Book Collection, Rikhardinkatu Library, Helsinki, Finland) and his *INTERSECTION* zine. He lives and works in New York City's Greenwich Village.

Miranda Stone began writing fiction as a child. She figured she was onto something when a relative asked why all her stories were so sad. Employing a minimalist writing style, her work is strongly influenced by the setting and culture of the Appalachian Mountains. Her short story "No One Is Invisible" was featured in the fourth issue of the literary journal *Parable Press*. Her other interests include genealogy, astronomy, and spending time in the mountains. She lives in Virginia.

Kent Tankersley is an American living in Helsinki, Finland, where he has worked in public relations and as a freelance travel writer. He has recently returned to writing fiction, an earlier passion of his, and has published stories in *KY Story, The Ante Review, Dew on the Kudzu*, and *Children, Churches and Daddies*, and elsewhere. He is also currently working on a screenplay and a sporadic blog about life as an expat. He has almost completely assimilated to his adopted home of Finland, but can barely speak the language. It's really tough.

Rose Yndigoyen is a freelance writer and archivist in New York City. She has written for the websites *AfterEllen* and *Biographile* and examines queer and feminist issues in pop culture on her blog, Queer for Theory. She is a co-creator and co-host of the podcast Pretty Little Recaps. Rose is a 2013 Lambda Literary fellow, and is hard at work on her first novel, a queer young adult love story. Rose lives with her wife in northern Manhattan. They are proud foster parents.

About NLSP 📖

We are New Lit Salon Press and we create books. We are writers. We are artists. We are makers with a mission: to publish the best and brightest, to amplify the voice of a generation lost in the void of a system concerned only about million dollar bestsellers. We look to the past but move boldly towards the future.

Founded by Brian Centrone (Publisher) and Jordan M. Scoggins (Creative Director) in 2012, New Lit Salon Press is based on the principle that Words and Art can and should coexist. NLSP is committed to publishing essays, stories, poems, novels, and art from undiscovered writers and promising artists who struggle to thrive in a marketplace that fails to recognize their talent. We believe in what you do.

The world of publishing is changing. NLSP not only recognises that but embraces it. To meet the demands of the evolving marketplace, NLSP releases are available on all major ebook platforms. However, because we are suckers for the printed page and we love the artistry of a physical object, we also produce print-on-demand trade editions of select titles.

With over 20 collective years of experience in creative, publishing, technology, and academic fields, we bring a unique skill set to the table. Our comprehensive approach is designed to nurture new and unheard talent in ways most indie publishers do not. We love what we do (and hope you do too).

We are artists. We are writers. We are NLSP and we create books.

Also available from ΠLSΡ📖

I Voted for Biddy Schumacher:
Mismatched Tales from the
Mind of Brian Centrone

Retrospective
by Michael Tice

Erotica
by Brian Centrone

Behind the Yellow Wallpaper:
New Tales of Madness
edited by Rose Yndigoyen

For more information visit
www.newlitsalonpress.com

CPSIA information can be obtained
at www.ICGtesting.com
Printed in the USA
LVHW021539010721
691686LV00022B/2801

9 780988 551275